Witch baby and me

Debi Gliori

CORGI BOOKS

WITCH BABY AND ME
A CORGI BOOK 978 0 552 55676 7

Published in Great Britain by Corgi Books,
an imprint of Random House Children's Books
A Random House Group Company

This edition published 2008

7 9 10 8

Set in Adobe Garamond Pro 14/14pt

Corgi Books are published by Random House Children's Books,
61–63 Uxbridge Road, London W5 5SA

www.**kids**at**random**house.co.uk

Addresses for companies within The Random House Group Limited
can be found at: www.randomhouse.co.uk/offices.htm

THE RANDOM HOUSE GROUP Limited Reg. No. 954009

A CIP catalogue record for this book is available from the British Library.

Printed and bound by CPI Group (UK) Ltd, Croydon, CR0 4YY

Also by Debi Gliori

PURE DEAD MAGIC
PURE DEAD WICKED
PURE DEAD BRILLIANT
DEEP TROUBLE
DEEP WATER
DEEP FEAR

Dedicated to families Great
and families Small but
especially to family Mine.

CONTENTS

IN THE TIME
BEFORE WITCH BABY

Wreathed in clouds in the coldest, wettest and most remote part of Scotland is an impossibly steep mountain called Ben Screeeiiighe. On its summit is a house so secret and hidden that nobody has even *heard* of it, let alone seen it. No postmen ever deliver mail to its rusting letterbox, no milkmen ever brave its crumbling doorstep and even the birds know better than to fly over its chimneys. What is this place? It is the lonely home of the Sisters of Hiss. Who are they? We know them by their other name of 'witches', but we know *nothing*.

We are, after all, only human.

We can have no idea what it must be like

to be four hundred years old like the Sisters
of Hiss.

We can only imagine what it must be

like to live on a mountain with only the wild wind and the snow for company.

Without a map, we can only guess at which of the many mountaintops in the coldest, rainiest and most remote bit of Scotland might be the one the Sisters call home.

We are, after all, only human.

But *some* humans are curious. They never stop trying to find out answers to questions. They're fascinated by hidden things. They want to find out everything there is to know about witches. They ask questions. They take photographs. They want to see the witches for themselves. Many of them have tried to find their way to where the witches live. Most of them have failed.

A few very determined humans have climbed all the way to the Sisters' front doorstep only to slip and fall off the edge –

Gosh, mind your step, slip, slither,
eeeeeeeeeek Yeeeeeaaar'
thud, thud,
splot.

A far, far smaller number of determined humans have made it to the Sisters' doorstep without slipping and falling and have even managed to open the letter box only to accidentally set off an avalanche –

Is there anybody at home,
yodel-ay-ee-hoo,
rumble, rumble, thunder,
crash, splat.

Some, I am sorry to say, have been found by the Sisters and turned into their dinner . . . or worse.

So. Better not be *too* curious. Better not ask too many questions. If you *ever* find a map that says:

O. S. Sheet 13. Version 6.6.6
Ben Screeeiiighe
&
The Sisters of Hiss

then for heaven's sake have the sense to put the map back where you found it. Forget you saw it. Promise you'll never go to the coldest, wettest and most remote part of Scotland, just on the off-chance that you might stumble upon the home of the Sisters of Hiss.

You Have Been Warned.

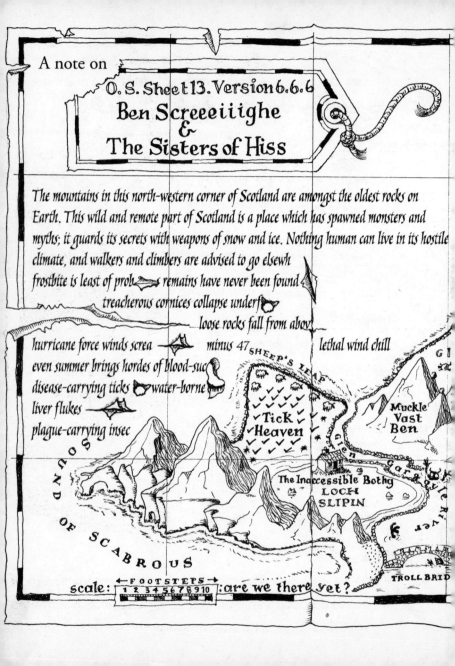

A note on

O. S. Sheet 13. Version 6.6.6
Ben Screeeiiighe
&
The Sisters of Hiss

The mountains in this north-western corner of Scotland are amongst the oldest rocks on Earth. This wild and remote part of Scotland is a place which has spawned monsters and myths; it guards its secrets with weapons of snow and ice. Nothing human can live in its hostile climate, and walkers and climbers are advised to go elsewh
frostbite is least of prob — remains have never been found
treacherous cornices collapse underf
loose rocks fall from abov
hurricane force winds screa — minus 47 — lethal wind chill
even summer brings hordes of blood-suc
disease-carrying ticks — water-borne
liver flukes
plague-carrying insec

SHEEP'S LEAP

Tick Heaven

Muckle Vast Ben

SOUND OF SCABROUS

The Inaccessible Bothy
LOCH SLIPIN

Glen Gargle

GI

ler RIVER

TROLL BRID

scale: ← FOOTSTEPS → 1 2 3 4 5 6 7 8 9 10 :are we there yet?

neb-na-cailleach

Ben Screeeiiighe(?)

CAPE CAILLEACH

slodan dubh

CHIN BAYYY

Wind Funnel

BAY OF JELLYFISH

GREAT TOAD GLACIER

Accident-Waiting-To-Happen-Ridge

Nervous

foothills of fffear

SLOW SANDS

Ben mout

Ben Eighh

LOCH OCHENLOCHINOCHINOCH

Ben Ow

QUICK SAND

Midge Central

Ben Ben Bhunn

CLAGGY SWAMP

impassible thicket

(This map was discovered in the glove compartment of an abandoned car, believed to belong to a hill walker who didn't return from an outing to Ben Screeeiiighe.)

THE SPAWNING OF
WITCH BABY

You can't just drop in to visit the Sisters of Hiss in their Highland hideaway unless you have a helicopter. This makes Ben Screeeiiighe the perfect place for the Sisters to live because they are very, very secretive and do not want any visitors, *especially* human ones. Human visitors drop litter all the way up the mountainside, take heaps of photographs, bang snow off their boots on the doorstep, peer through the letter box, ask endless stupid questions, demand to use the bathroom and forget to close the front door behind them when they leave.

After centuries of putting up with such bad behaviour, the Sisters have decided that humans are no good for anything except firewood. Few trees can grow on mountaintops, so firewood that generously hauls itself up the mountain and walks through your front door is terrifically useful.

Listen, over the **shriek** of the wind –

'Throw another human on the fire, there's a dear.'

Ghastly smoke flies up the Sisters' chimneys and is immediately whisked away in the wind.

Tonight, the full moon is playing peek-a-boo, weaving in and out of ribbons of black clouds scudding across the sky. It is, as they say, a dark and stormy night. A night for hatching plans of great wickedness.

It is the perfect night for spawning the Witch Baby.

Inside the Sisters' home, it is every bit as gloomy as you might expect. The Sisters do not possess a vacuum cleaner. They do not realize such things have been invented. They have lived on their mountain for four hundred years, after all. Mounds of soot, layers of dust and ropes of cobwebs cover every surface of their house in a sticky veil. Shrivelled brown flowers droop from dismal vases and all is dark and dank. Even the Sisters' lamps and lanterns seem to give out darkness instead of light. Smoke from the strangling fire puffs into the room and swirls about the ceiling.

Gathered around the fire are the Sisters of Hiss. These are three women of spectacular ugliness. One has an enormous nose like a meat-hook, another has a chin you could use to slice bread and the third is covered with so many warts she looks like a toad.[*]

Hanging from the walls all around the room are mirrors. Big mirrors, small ones, some with priceless golden frames, some with cheap wooden ones. Sadly, they're all useless. Every single one of the mirrors is cracked from side to side, shattered by the Sisters' attempts to look at their reflections.

Listen – there goes another one.

'Mirror, mirror, on the wall, who's the fair— **CRACKKKKKK. Oh, HISSSSSSS.'**

Oh, ugly, ugly, mirror-cracking Sisters. None of them will marry a handsome

---

* Ooops. My mistake. She is a toad. She's the one who had the unfortunate accident that we're not allowed to talk about.

prince. Oh, ancient, ancient wrinkly Sisters.

They are too old to be mummies, too scary to be grannies, but that doesn't stop them wanting what they cannot have.

More than anything in the whole world, the Sisters of Hiss want a little Witch Baby of their own.

They have always dreamed of having a tiny little baby to hold in their arms. A tiny little baby who wouldn't look at them and go, **'Eeeeugh.'** A tiny little baby who would grow up to become a Daughter of Hiss. Poor Sisters. All they really want is to be loved, despite their chins, noses and warts.

At first, they filled their hidden house at the top of Ben Screeeiiighe with things they thought a baby would like; knitted hats and shawls, a pram and a high chair. Then they waited for a baby to appear.

Years passed, but no baby appeared. The shawls and hats were eaten by moths, the pram rusted and the high chair crumbled with woodworm, but no baby came to the house on the mountain. After many, many years went by, the Sisters decided to take matters into their own hands. They came up with a Plan to spawn a Witch Baby. No handsome prince would be needed, just a baby. A *human* baby.

The Plan also needs a full moon, a big storm, some dark inky clouds, and the sun has to be in the sign of the Bull. The Sisters have had to wait for this to come together for years: some nights there's a full moon but the clouds are pink and fluffy – perfect for spawning dear little bunnies, but useless for Witch Babies. Some nights there's a moon, a storm, even some inky clouds, but the sun is in the sign of the Toad – don't ask.

But tonight, close to midnight on the twelfth of May, the Sisters' faces glow with delight. They are clustered around their fireplace, almost fizzing with excitement.

For tonight's *The Night*.

Tonight the weather, the moon and the planets are all conspiring to create the perfect conditions for The Spawning.

Woo-hoOO.

Here she comes, the Witch Baby.

MAKING BABY

The Nose begins to fan the fire with her skirts until a tiny curl of flame jumps out of the ashes in the hearth. She fans some more, her bony elbows pumping up and down and her skirt flapping like a sail. The flames grow and leap, reaching up the chimney's throat and trying to climb up and out into the storm. A sudden down-draught swirls the ashes in the hearth and makes the Nose sneeze loudly.

All at once the fireplace fills with white smoke.

The smoke smells awful – of burned pumpkins and dragon's underwear. Coughing and gagging, the Sisters retreat to the other side of the room, but they never take their gaze away from the fireplace. This is because in the middle of the smoke, a picture is forming. It's a very small picture, but despite its size, the Sisters can see it's a picture of babies. Lots of babies in little plastic cots. Is this a baby factory? An orphanage? No. It's a hospital nursery for newborns. It is Baby Central. The Sisters' hearts beat a little faster. If all goes according to plan, one of those babies will become their very own Witch Baby.

The Chin seizes the fireside poker and points it towards the white smoke. Amazing! The poker works like a television's remote control. Suddenly the image of babies is clearer, bigger and much easier to see. And now, over the howl of the wind and the crackling of the fire, comes the sound of babies crying.

'**Wahhh**,' they go. '**Wah, wahhh**.'

Poor little things. They're frightened something awful is about to happen.

They're probably right. It is.

The Toad hops towards the fireplace and points a webbed foot towards a baby who is sobbing louder than all the others put together. Smoke surrounds this baby in a circle that swirls and swoops and finally re-forms into an arrow, as if to say, THIS one. Choose her. Through

the swirling smoke, the Toad can read a little
pink card at the end of the baby's cot. A little
pink card that says:

Daisy Macrae
12.00 P.M. May 12th

The baby falls silent, gazing wide-eyed as
the gigantic shadow of a warty toad crosses
her cot. In their darkly lit room, hundreds of
miles to the north, the Sisters nod in approval.
Very good. Baby Daisy MacRae is not afraid of
warty toads. One by one, shadows appear and
fall across Baby Daisy's cot; a gigantic hooked
nose followed by a chin so sharp it cleaves the
darkness in two. The baby opens her mouth
and gurgles.

The Sisters inhale sharply. It has begun. A look of deep concentration crosses the baby's face, and a loud **prrr-atta-tat-tat** sound comes drumming out of her nappy. The Sisters smile. This is exactly the sound they were hoping to hear. Switching from being a human to being a Hiss involves lots of magical rewiring. This causes lots of gas to form inside a baby's tummy and that, as we all know, can be embarrassingly loud. It can also be somewhat dangerous. If there is a blockage somewhere that prevents this gas from escaping, well . . . anything could happen. The baby might explode or it could even turn purple and start shooting sparks out of its bottom. However, the **prrr-atta-tat-tat** coming from Daisy MacRae's bottom is proof positive that the Witch Baby spell is working perfectly. Soon, Daisy's blue eyes will turn green and her tiny rosebud mouth will flush with a deeper shade of pink than before, but the real changes that are taking place inside Daisy will be invisible to the naked eye.

One by one, the Sisters work through their to-do list of Witch Baby spell-checks:

a) Engage wart-mode. This is a magical tweak to Daisy's DNA[*], which will make sure that when she reaches the grand old age of forty-eight, she will sprout thousands of warts on her nose, toes and chin.

b) Activate tonsil-tweak. This is a tightening of Daisy's vocal cords, which will make her voice slightly squeaky and quavery. While she is only a baby, or even a young child, nobody will notice, but when Daisy attains adulthood, she will begin to sound like a witch.

[*] We are all made from this stuff. Whatever it is. Ask your mother to explain.

c) Memory overwrite. For this, the Sisters have to download twenty point seven four terabytes of alchemic RAM with full cross-platform functionality and added value hyperlink protocol.*

d) Meaningless muttering. This goes something like – gobble dee gook, bah-bah ramdass, aw minny, aw minny, tea mo tay, tea mo tay, cham-pu.

There. Done. It's the best spell the Sisters of Hiss have ever cast. The Nose blows on the fire, the Chin fans the white smoke back up the chimney, and the Toad scrapes a spell-over symbol in the fire's embers with a poker.

Outside, the wind howls louder, and a blizzard swirls around the mountaintops.

Woo-hoo. Something wicked this way comes.

* No. Me either. I'm hoping it doesn't hurt.

In the city hospital two hundred miles south, Baby Daisy MacRae shyly attempts her first spell. Slowly she floats up to the ceiling. Slowly she crosses the nursery full of babies, dips down through the door and out along the corridor. Amazingly, no one notices that there's a brand-new baby floating across the ceiling. No one in the hospital looks up to see Baby

Daisy hovering outside a door at the far end of the corridor. Slowly the door opens to reveal a shape asleep in a bed. Baby Daisy MacRae gives a tiny sigh of happiness, flies across the room, slips under the covers and curls up beside her new mummy.

Witch Baby has arrived. Woo-hOO.

As if in agreement, the wind chooses this moment to blow a gust straight down the chimney. Woo, hOOooo, it goes. Immediately the fire goes out and a huge puff of ash billows out of the grate. Choking and coughing, the Sisters peer into the fireplace, where a new picture is forming in the swirling dust.

Baby Daisy MacRae has turned herself into a dragon and lies in her cot, happily blowing fire-bubbles. Baby Daisy's big sister is *not* a dragon and, judging by the horrified look on

her face, has never *seen* a dragon at such close quarters before. On either side of the cot stand Daisy's proud parents and, behind them, a scowling older boy, all unaware that they have a fire-breathing dragon in their midst. All, that is, except for Baby Daisy's sister.

'Muuuuuuum,' wails Baby Daisy's sister. 'The baby's turned into a *dragon*!'

'Lily, don't be silly. Daisy's just a baby.'

'But, Muuuuuum,' Lily insists, pulling back Daisy's quilt to expose a pair of wings and a long, whippy tail. 'Can't you see?'

'That's quite enough, young lady,' says Lily and Daisy's dad. 'Anyone can see that your little sister is a baby, not a mythical fire-breathing beast. I know it's hard when a new baby comes along, but I'm sure you'll grow to love your little sister . . .'

'I didn't,' mutters the scowling older boy, glaring at Lily.

'Thanks a bunch,' mutters Lily.

'Jack,' warns Dad.

'Children,' sighs Mum.

'**Wahhhhh**,' wails Daisy. Instantly, the spell is broken and Daisy is turned back into a baby. A baby in a black babygro with a health warning written across its chest.

Back home with the Sisters of Hiss, the mood is turning ugly.

'I thought nothing could go wrong with this spell. I thought our Witch Baby was supposed to be a secret.' The Toad is hopping up and down in front of the fireplace, her webbed feet leaving little pockmarks in the ashes.

'Calm down,' the Chin says, but the Toad isn't listening. She's working herself into a frenzy. Her warty wattles quiver with outrage.

'This is *dreadful*. Awful. *Diabolical*. If the Witch Baby's sister can see that she's a witch, then our cover is blown. This is a *disaster*.'

The Chin says nothing, but looks longingly at the poker. You can tell she would dearly love to use it for something other than prodding the fire.

Outside, a new day is dawning. Sleet peppers the windows and the wind dies down to a dull shriek.

'I have to agree with the Toad,' sniffs the Nose, dabbing at her nostrils with a corner of her sleeve. 'It does appear that we have made a dreadful Spelling Mistake.'

The Toad shudders. Spelling Mistakes are awful. This one could turn out to be the worst they've ever made. This one could be even worse than the Spelling Mistake ~~which turned her into a Toad~~ we don't talk about.*

So. The Toad takes a deep, steadying breath and begins to explain exactly why this Spelling Mistake is such a terrible disaster.

'That . . . that Lily will blow our cover. She's not stupid – it won't take her very long to work out what manner of creature her baby sister has become. Mark my words, once she's twigged that her sister is a witch, then she'll tell the whole world. First her parents, then her brother, then her teacher, her classmates, the postman, the milkman . . . everyone will know. Meanwhile, our Witch Baby will be casting

---

* Okay? OKAY? Read the Toad's warty green lips.
  We. Don't. Go. There.

spells all over the place, giving the impression that it's so easy to become a witch, why, even a baby can do it. Right?'

'**Ughhh**,' groans the Nose. 'By this time next year there won't be a frog left unkissed in Scotland. Pointy hats will sell out from John o' Groats to Jock's Lodge.

Before we know it, there'll be field trips to Ben Screeeiiighe to spot witches in their natural habitat. They'll make television documentaries, films . . .'

'Exactly,' croaks the Toad, her bulging eyes almost falling out of her head with the horror of it all.

'They'll teach Witchcraft in schools,' the Nose continues gloomily. 'Someone'll write a bestselling book about it . . . then the whole wide world will beat a path to our door . . .'

'I think we can do something about that,' says the Chin, smiling unpleasantly. 'The baby is very young. She will not develop her full powers or her voice until much later. Her spells will be weak and easily broken. She will only be able to do one at a time, and they won't last long. Every time she cries, as babies do, her magic will fail. She won't be able to tell anyone what fun it is to be a witch for a long time. And as for Lily: I suspect that nobody will believe her. If nobody else can see that her baby sister is a witch, it will simply appear as if Lily's making it all up. So . . . let's not be too hasty. Time is on our side, dear Sisters. We can afford to wait and see if Lily really is a danger to our way of life, and if so, we have more than enough time to arrange for her to have a little . . . accident.'

'Sssso,' hisses the Nose, turning her back to the fireplace, 'you're saying that our secret is safe for now. Only the Witch Baby's sister can see what's really going on, but—'

'Why?' interrupts the Toad, her voice quivering like toadspawn. 'Nobody has given me a reason why Lily can see what Daisy is. I thought only Hiss Sisters could see other witches.'

'Yesssss,' sighs the Chin. 'And then again, no. It's true that most humans wouldn't recognize a witch if she bit them on the leg—'

'Ewww, what a hideous thought,' mutters the Nose.

'Most humans are blind to the presence of magic,' the Chin continues wearily. 'But very occasionally you get a kid who is brave, plays a musical instrument, likes Brussels sprouts—'

'**WHAAAT?**' splutters the  Toad. 'That's imposs—'

'Don't interrupt,' snaps the Chin. 'As I was saying, once in a blue moon a cluster of these weird kids will appear and then our secret will be a secret no longer. Our Witch Baby's sister Lily is one.' The Chin pauses to sniff in disgust before adding, 'She won't be a problem, though. Nobody ever listens to her, so no matter how many times she tries to tell her parents about our Witch Baby, they won't believe her. Everyone will assume she's making up stories about the new baby because she's jealous. It's not Lily I'm worried about. I'm far more worried that there are others like her out there.'

Silence falls. The Nose and the Toad don't dare speak. Finally the Chin shudders and carries on. 'Put it this way. If another one of these children comes along and sees that she's a Witch Baby, we're in trouble. But don't worry. It may never happen. There's only a one-in-a-million chance that another one of these kids will appear. Trust me, it'll all work out.'

There is a brief silence, then:

'**Pffffff**,' mutters the Toad. 'Last time you said that, look what happened to me.'

Poor Toad. Poor Sisters, too. All they want is a little Witch Baby of their very own. Instead, they've made Daisy. Who knows what will happen now?

For a long time, not a lot *does* happen. At least, not when anyone's looking. After all, nobody notices what Daisy does in her cot at night when her family is sleeping. Fortunately for Daisy, nobody notices the scorch-marks on the roof; nor do they spot her little baby footprints

on the kitchen
ceiling. Meanwhile,
Daisy has her first
birthday, her big brother Jack has his twelfth,
her big sister Lily turns nine and the whole
family moves house.

Hundreds of miles to the north, in their secret
home on top of Ben Screeeiiighe, the Nose,
the Toad and the Chin watch and wait. The
Sisters do not celebrate birthdays and they have
no intention of moving house ever. Not unless
things go disastrously wrong, that is . . .

One:

Right. Let's get this bit over with very quickly because I may not have much time left. Three minutes ago, my name was Lily MacRae and I was nine years, two months and three days old. Three minutes ago, I lived in the Old Station House in a tiny village in the Highlands of Scotland. We only moved in a few weeks ago, but the minute I walked through the front door I knew I didn't want to live here. Nobody I know lives here and I miss my old friends so much it hurts. I want to go back and live in our lovely old house in Edinburgh, but that's not going to happen. Not now that we've moved to the quietest, loneliest, most boring place in the whole world. Which means that unless I want to die of loneliness, I'm going to have to make new friends.

New friends, new house, and a new life. Same family, though. I live with Mum and Dad and my big brother Jack and – flash of lightning, roll of thunder – My Baby Sister. That's sister with an extra hiss. SissSSter.

So, four minutes ago, Mum sat up in her coffin, her red eyes glowing and blood dripping off her fangs, and said, 'Take your SissSSter Draculina out for a quick bite, would you, Lily?'

Actually, I made that bit up. Four minutes ago, Mum said, 'Lily, be a darling. I need to make some very long and boring phone calls and Daisy needs her nap. Could you please take her into the garden and see if you can get her to sleep?'

Two things I want to point out here. First of all: Daisy. My baby sister is the least Daisy-ish baby in the whole wide world. If Mum and  Dad had to pick a flowery name, why didn't they pick Cactus? Or Venus Fly Trap? Or even Nettle? But Daisy? That's a bit like calling your pet shark Nibbles.

The other thing is that I stand more chance of getting Daisy to fly than getting her to sleep. Mum can't get her to sleep, Dad can't get her to sleep, I can't get her to sleep – but put her anywhere near my big brother Jack, and Daisy's eyes roll back in her head and . . . she's gone. Fast asleep in seconds. How does Jack do it? Simple. Jack grunts a lot, turns up his music and goes, tss, tss, tss, in answer to everything*:

---

* This is so boring it even makes me want to go to sleep.

More pudding, Jack?

TSS, TSSS, TSS.

Don't you think you're going to damage your ears having your music turned up like that?

TSS, TSSS, TSS.

The-Earth-is-about-to-be-blown-up-by-Martians-and-you-have-three-seconds-left-before-you-turn-into-a-cinder.

TSS, TSSS, TSS.

Anyway. Three minutes ago, I was me. Me, Lily MacRae, pushing my little sister Daisy round the garden in her pram. That was then. This is now. And now . . . now, I think I'm about to die of embarrassment.

Why? Because two minutes ago, my little baby sister turned me into a – I can hardly bear to say it – a . . . a . . . *slug*. One minute I was wheeling her around the garden making go-to-sleep-Daisy noises, and the next minute I was on the ground, slithering along on my tummy. I didn't even realize I'd changed into a slug until I caught sight of my reflection in a puddle.

'**Eeeeew**,' I screamed, and then,

'OHHHHH **NOOOOO**.'

I'm black and slimy. How on earth am I supposed to make new friends like that?

Hi. My name's Lily and— **Ooops** . . . squirt . . . forget it. I'll just slither away and get on with dying of embarrassment.

From now on, my life will be all about eating raw cabbage and squeezing slime out of my bottom. This sounds like a **Fate Worse Than**

Death. I hate cabbage. When Mum and Dad come looking for me and Daisy, first thing they'll say is, 'Where has Lily gone? Fancy running off and leaving poor Daisy all alone. Poor little baby, awwwwwww . . .'

And then, 'Eeeeew. There's a slug under Daisy's pushchair. How disgusting.'

I hope they won't hurl me in the pond or over

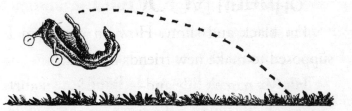

the hedge into the next-door garden. I mean, I might die. Killed by my very own loving mum and dad. I want to scream, IT'S SOOO NOT FAIR, at the top of my lungs, but I'm not even sure if slugs have lungs . . .

Daisy has lungs, though. Boy, does she have lungs. She is so loud.

I slither backwards to get a better look. **Squuuirt, squuuirt, sliiither**, I go.

'WAY LILY GONE?' she roars. 'WayYYY LILY?'

Oh, dear. Daisy gets louder when she's cross. She thinks I've vanished. If I wasn't a slug, I could soon cheer her up. But right now all I can do is squirt and slither and cover her in slime. Poor Daisy. Poor me, too.

I've had fourteen months of Daisy the Witch Baby, but it's not getting any easier. You probably think I'd be used to her witchy ways by now, but I'm not. Every time she casts a spell, it takes me by surprise, and not in a good way. Take the first time I saw her. It was the day Dad took Jack and me to the hospital to see Mum and our new baby, Daisy. The new baby lay in a little cot beside Mum's bed. I was really excited. I couldn't *wait* to hold her. I bent over the cot and there she was, Baby Daisy, gazing at the ceiling with her big golden eyes. I had about two seconds to notice she had a pair of wings folded under her spine, a tail curled neatly beside her hind legs, and flames flickering in and out of her nostrils, before her big eyes swivelled in my direction and I screamed:

'Muuuuuuum. The baby's turned into a *dragon*!'

That was the moment my life changed for ever. Because first Mum, then Dad and then even Jack turned to me and said, 'Don't be silly, Lily. Daisy's not a dragon, she's a baby.'

Excuse me? Anyone could see the baby wasn't human, couldn't they?

I looked at Daisy. Daisy blinked her golden eyes, burped out a tiny flame and burst into tears. Immediately, she changed back. Into my little baby sister. I blinked. Had I just seen that? Was I dreaming?

'Here,' said Dad, 'why don't you hold her? Give your new baby sister a little cuddle. Go on. She won't bite – ha ha ha.'

I was terrified. Dad knew nothing. What if she turned into a dragon again? Or worse? I risked a peek at the heavy bundle Dad had put in my arms. It wasn't a dragon. It was a very small baby. A very small baby in a black babygro with something written across its front.

Warning Hazardous Material.
This is a genuine Witch Baby.
Do not attempt to adjust, alter or
meddle with its destiny.
YOU HAVE BEEN WARNED.

There. In black and white. The proof that I wasn't dreaming.

'Dad, look. *Look*. It says on her front. "Witch Baby". *There*. See? Told you so.'

'LILY.' Dad sounded cross. 'That's enough of that Witch Baby nonsense. Time for us to go home and let Mum and Daisy get some sleep.'

'But . . . but, Dad. LOOK.' I couldn't believe it. Was he *blind*? What was going on? There it was, in big white letters on Daisy's babygro. Wasn't it? I checked. Sure enough, there were the big white letters, but now they said:

Hush-a-bye

'That was a bit risky, wasn't it?' said the Chin. 'What if someone had believed Lily?'

43

'Poor child. Aren't we being a bit mean?' demanded the Toad, whose heart was far more tender than those of her Sisters.

'Mean, schmean,' sniffed the Nose. 'You can't make an omelette without breaking a few frying pans. Besides,' she added with a smirk, 'think about it. No one ever listens to children. Especially not when they're telling the truth. The more Lily tries to tell everybody about Daisy, the safer our little secret becomes. I tell you, Sisters, our plan is perfect. Nothing can possibly go wrong.'

Dad, Jack and I drove home in silence. I was stunned. I couldn't believe what had just happened. Was I going mad? I was so sure I'd seen our new baby turn into a dragon, but nobody else had seen *anything*.

Worse was to come. From that day on, I

never knew what version of Daisy was going to
be waiting for me inside her cot. One day she
was a baby frog, squatting on her quilt. The
next, she was a little eel, slipping out of my
arms and coiling across the floor like a snake.

The day after, a tiny crocodile, snapping at my arm with her gummy jaws. Baby footprints appeared where no footprints should have been, but only I could see them. Sometimes Daisy smelled of bonfires, but no one else noticed. In the middle of all this weirdness, there was one thing I was one hundred per cent sure about. Whatever Daisy was, she certainly wasn't a normal baby.

Mum *still* didn't notice, nor did Dad, so I tried to convince my big brother Jack that Daisy was a witch, but I could tell he wasn't listening. Actually, he couldn't hear a word I was saying because he had his earbuds in. I could have danced up and down in front of him pulling faces like a gargoyle and he would just have smiled and nodded as he shut his bedroom door in my face.

Mum didn't listen either. She got a faraway

look in her eyes and said it would Take Time To Adjust To The New Baby. Poor Mum. She knows nothing. Fourteen months have passed and I *still* haven't adjusted. I mean, I love Daisy to bits, but how am I ever supposed to adjust to sharing my life with a witch, even if she is a little teeny-weeny one? Under her pink babygro lies a junior member of the Society of Women with Pointy Hats, Chin Warts and Spelling Issues. If this was a film of My Life, there would be a roll of thunder, a flash of lightning and a distant scream. My little sister is – gasp – a Witch Baby.

And nobody knows it but me.

Crashhh, flashhhh, eee-eee-EEE.

Two:

The problem with Witch Baby,
by Lily (a.k.a. The Slug)

The thing is, witches aren't like us. Not deep inside, where it counts. Witch Baby looks like one of us: she has two green eyes, one little button nose and the correct number of arms and legs in all the right places. Just like you and me. But that's where it ends. Between her ears, in the place where we have a brain, Witch Baby has a . . .

Well, actually, I have no *idea* what she's got in there, but whatever it is, it's nothing like a normal baby brain.

How do I know? Let me explain. Normal babies are happy sitting on their bottoms, picking things up off the floor – balls, bricks, bluebottles – and sticking them straight into their mouths. Sometimes they go Num-num-num if the bluebottle was really tasty. That's normal babies we're talking about, not Witch Babies. My Witch Baby doesn't pick things up. At least, not when she thinks nobody's looking. When she thinks no one can see her, she stares, claps her hands, and then whatever she wants to pick up comes floating through the air towards her.

Sounds pretty cool, huh? Trust me, it isn't. Take yesterday. Yesterday she wanted the fridge. Luckily Mum was upstairs unpacking, so she didn't see what happened. I did, though. I turned my back on Witch Baby for a nano-second . . . and caught sight of the biscuit tin.

The open biscuit tin with one lonely Kit-Kat finger inside. I'm not exactly sure what happened next, but I'm sure I heard that Kit-Kat speak. I'm positive it said (very quietly) so that only I could hear: Go on, eat me now.

Well. What was I supposed to do?

Exactly. So, licking my chocolate-covered fingers to remove the evidence, I turned back and there was Witch Baby, giggling. . . and there was the fridge, *floating* right above my head.

YIKES.

I couldn't scream, in case I startled Witch Baby and she forgot that she was holding the fridge over my head with nothing stronger than the Power of her Thoughts. Powerful as they are, Daisy's thoughts (or spells, to give them their proper name) can be broken by Daisy bursting into tears or being distracted. Some of her spells s . . . l . . . o . . . w . . . l . . . y fade away to nothing, and others vanish instantly. So, for instance, if the spell holding the fridge in the air were to vanish instantly, I would be a very Squished Lily. However, if I distract Daisy rather then startling her, there's a good chance she might put the fridge down, rather than drop it.

'Wah-woo-wuh?' I said. My voice had gone all wobbly. I tried again. 'Woo-woo-would you like a biscuit?'

Witch Baby's eyes narrowed a fraction. The fridge stopped floating and became very still. Almost as if it was waiting for something.

'Biccit?'

Before we go any further, I should explain that Witch Baby is a person of few words. She can say all the usual baby words like **Mumma, Dadda, wantit, wantit now, biccit, no likeit dat.** As well as these, Witch Baby has a few more words not normally spoken by small persons in nappies. Words like **full moon** and **magic**; **wolfbane** and **toadspawn**. If you listen very carefully, you can just about understand what she's trying to say: **boomstek, WayWoof** and **vampie.**

You have to listen very hard, though. For some reason, Mum and Dad are no good at listening properly – they never seem to hear what Daisy is saying. 'Ahhhh,' they coo, 'listen to Daisy. She's saying woof. Are you playing at being our little puppy? Ahhhh, bless. Does it want a doggy biccit?'

Biscuits. That reminded me. I was about to be squished under the fridge all because of a biscuit.

'Not biccit,' my would-be murderer decided. 'Not likeit, dat. Want udder one.'

The fridge quivered slightly, and so did I. Udder one? What other one?

'Cat-Cat. Wantit.'

Oh, dear. This was Very Bad News indeed. She meant she wanted the last Kit-Kat. Which was inside my tummy along with two slices of toast and peanut butter, one bowl of cornflakes and half a banana. Sadly, the Kit-Kat was non-returnable. At least not in any form that Witch Baby would enjoy.

'Wantit biccit. Wantit nowwwwww.'

And now Witch Baby's face was turning as red as the wrapper of the biscuit she wanted. My legs turned to jelly. Help. I was in big trouble. I was in the deepest of deep poo. I might be about to die for lack of a chocolate biscuit. My life flashed before my eyes, including the last ten million

times I've heard Witch Baby throw a wobbly. And then I remembered two very important rules I've learned about what to do when Witch Babies throw wobblies.

RULE NUMBER ONE: it may seem unkind, but try to *ignore* the fact your baby is going purple and turning itself into a cross between a boiled goblin and a shriek alarm. Being ignored will teach Baby that throwing a wobbly is very boring and does not get results.

RULE NUMBER TWO: Witch Babies can only do one spell at a time, so if you need to break a spell, try to *distract* your baby. Offer it something else to play with. Babies like objects that are bright, shiny and noisy, especially if they belong to other people and are accompanied by the words, NO – DON'T *TOUCH* THAT.

The rules work very well. Almost too well.

'No, Daisy,' I said. 'Whatever you do, don't

touch Mum's very precious, sparkly glass bowl.'
I may even have added an 'Oooo' for effect.
Anyway, that was how Witch Baby grew bored
with playing with the fridge, put it back down,
made the precious, sparkly bowl fly and learned
how loudly Mum can shriek.

'NOOOOOO!' shrieked Mum. 'PUT
MY ANTIQUE CRYSTAL PUNCH BOWL
DOWN RIGHT NOW!'

CrashhhHHHHHHHH.

Tinkle. Shatter.

Three:
A little bit of slug

I don't know if
Daisy really meant
to turn me into a
slug, but it doesn't
matter. The fact is,

I am a mollusc and I will remain a mollusc
unless I find a way to break the spell and turn
back into me. How? I have no idea. I'm only a
slug. I have slithered and slipped up the wheel,
crawled along the shopping tray and hauled
myself onto the handle of Daisy's pushchair,
but it's no good. I can't distract Daisy because
I have no voice, no legs, no hands and no way
of grabbing hold of my little sister and yelling,
'OK – ENOUGH ALREADY. HA HA HA.
SO FUNNY. NOT. NOW STOP.'

Not that she'd listen. She's too busy going, 'LILY LILY LIIIILY,' and rocking from side to side in her pushcha—

Uh-oh.

We're moving. The pushchair's wheels are turning. We're rolling downhill. The garden behind the Old Station House slopes down to a pond. This is bad news because we're hurtling towards the pond and I can't make us stop. Slugs can't work brakes. Now Daisy has gone quiet. This may be because we're going so fast her face is pinned back against her pushchair and she can't prise her lips apart to scream any more. If I wasn't a slug, I'd be screaming, LOOK OUT! HERE COMES THE POND!

We're going to dieeeeeee– SPLASH!

And finally, WAHHHHHHHHHHH.

Fortunately, the water in the pond only comes up to my knees, and if Daisy can wail, then obviously she isn't drowning either. We're alive. WE'RE ALIVE!

Hang on a minute.

I look at Witch Baby.

She looks back at me and stops going WAHHH.

'Oh, Lilil,' she says, then she gives a little cackle and claps her chubby hands with delight. 'Wheeee SPLASH!' she says, obviously feeling very pleased with herself. 'Whee, whee, way is WayWoof?'

Ah. WayWoof. I wondered when we'd get round to him.

Four:
Enter WayWoof

Listen. The Chin and the Toad are having an argument. Inside their house, glasses shatter and raised voices shriek, crackle and croak. Sparks fly up their chimney into the darkness.

'That blasted *dog*. It's all your fault!' the Chin bawls.

'I wasn't the one who opened the front door,' whines the Toad.

'No, but *you* should have stopped it.'

'But . . . but I *couldn't*,' bleats the Toad. 'It was the day after we'd found our Witch Baby. I was tired. I wasn't thinking straight. The dog ran straight past me. By the time I reached it—'

'Yes, yes, yes. We've all heard it a thousand times. By the time you managed to drag your warty old lazybones out of your chair and hobbled after the dog, it had leaped into the fireplace—'

'What could I have done to stop it?' The Toad is nearly in tears. 'How was I to know that the ashes were still full of magic from the night before? I mean, come *on*. The dog just seemed to vanish up the chimney—'

'And the damage was done,' interrupted the

Nose. 'And no amount of argument can undo it.'

A deep silence falls. The Sisters shiver at the memory.

'Throw another human on the fire, dear,' begs the Chin. 'There's a chill in the air tonight.'

WayWoof is Daisy's invisible dog. Imagine a cross between a dog, a wolf and a dustbin, and that's WayWoof. Daisy and I can see WayWoof, but Mum, Dad and Jack can't. He looks like a dog, howls like a wolf and smells far worse than a dustbin. I have no idea why he smells so bad, but he does. Sorry, WayWoof.

On the day we brought Mum and Baby Daisy home from the hospital, WayWoof moved in. At first nobody noticed him, because we were busy playing with our new baby. But WayWoof was busy too. He was busy making smells all over our house. As we ooh-ed and ahh-ed over Baby Daisy, WayWoof was making pongs in the kitchen, silent-but-deadlies in the bathroom and stenches in the hall.

I didn't know it was WayWoof making all the smells. I couldn't see him properly at first. Then, he looked like a patch of shadow moving

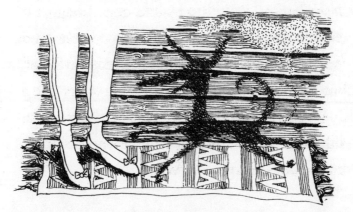

across the floor. I think Daisy was too small to magic him properly. Brand-new Witch Babies probably have to learn how to do spells, just like they have to learn how to do everything else.

So, for a little while, I had no idea where the awful whiffs were coming from. Secretly, I blamed Daisy's nappy. But to be honest, I hardly thought about the smell because shortly after Daisy was born, Mum and Dad decided it was time for us to move house. To my horror, they said we were all going to move to a house a long, long way from Edinburgh. *Two hundred miles away*. I couldn't believe it at first. I was going to move two hundred miles away from my best friends, Ally, Jen and Frieda? I'd never see them again?

Did this mean I was going to miss Ally's birthday party?

Yes.

Who would Jen tell all her deepest secrets to after I left?

Someone else.

And Frieda? I'd never find a friend who made me laugh like she did.

Never.

This was the worst thing that had ever happened. I was furious with Mum and Dad for doing this to me. I cried myself to sleep for a month.

My eyes went all puffy and my nose was so bunged up with all the crying that I couldn't smell anything at all, not even WayWoof. Not that I knew he even existed, back then. However, one night, a few weeks before the Big Move, I heard Daisy in her cot, laughing as if she was being tickled.

'Hahahahaha,' she giggled. 'Wayoo, Wayoo, Wayoo.'

I stuck my head into her room and saw
WayWoof.

'**EEEEE**,' I screamed. 'There's a huge
DOG in Daisy's room!'

Problem was, nobody but me and Witch
Baby could see him. Mum said I was probably
having nightmares about our Big Move because
she couldn't see any dogs in Daisy's bedroom,
and besides, it was past midnight and could we
all please go back to sleep? When she'd stomped
back to bed, Dad came to tuck me in and said
maybe the reason I could see WayWoof and he

couldn't was because I was born under a blue moon. Jack said something very rude, but he couldn't see Way-Woof either. Mind you, WayWoof could have been a thirteen-metre fire-snorting dragon with diarrhoea and Jack still wouldn't have noticed him. But guess what? Even though they couldn't see Way-Woof, they could *smell* him just fine. And guess who they thought was making the terrible smells?

'Oh, *dear*,' Mum said, fanning the air in

front of her face. 'Bit of an upset tummy, Lily darling?'

Dad went for the straight-to-the-point, no-nonsense, direct approach. '*LILY.* For heaven's sake. Was that you?'

So embarrassing. So unfair. Sometimes I feel as if I'm an alien that's landed in the middle of a nice, ordinary Earth family.[*]

Nobody else in my family (apart from Daisy, obviously) can tell that Daisy is a Witch Baby.

Nobody else in my family was born under a blue moon.[**]

Nobody else in my family (apart from Daisy) can see WayWoof.

WayWoof has his good points, though. For one thing, Witch Baby loves him to bits. When she sees him, she wraps her arms round WayWoof's hairy neck, closes her eyes and

[*] Nice and ordinary, except for the youngest family member who happens to be a Witch baby, but let's not quibble.

[**] Whatever *that* is.

makes little
cooing sounds.
In return, Way-
Woof closes his
eyes and pants. It's hard
to tell if this means WayWoof is
enjoying himself because he closes his eyes and
pants a lot of the time.

Another good thing about WayWoof is
that when *he's* around, Daisy can't cast any
spells. WayWoof needs Daisy to concentrate
on him or he just fades away to nothing. When
WayWoof is absent, I start to worry that
Daisy's Up To No Good. WayWoof is like an
early-warning incoming-spell alarm. As long as
WayWoof is around, I can relax and breathe easy.

No. I didn't mean that.

Breathe easy is the *last* thing I can do
when WayWoof appears. I need a gas mask

to breathe when he's around. But at least, if I can see him, that means I'm safe from Daisy turning me into a slug, or worse. And here comes WayWoof now, galloping towards us, tongue lolling and a tell-tale cloud of gas trailing from his tail end. If he wasn't so stinky, he'd really be very sweet. Daisy and I are soaking wet from falling in the pond, but WayWoof doesn't mind. He's delighted to see us, no matter what state we're in. Which is more than can be said for Mum. Just as I realize how much mud

is clinging to Daisy and me, Mum appears.

'There you are, my poppets,' she says. Then she notices the mess. Slimy pond-weed drips from the pushchair, Daisy looks like she's been dipped in poo up to her middle, and my best pink T-shirt looks like a giant blew his nose on it. To make things even worse, WayWoof immediately sits down and lets rip.

Mum blinks rapidly, then coughs, but I'm not sure if that's because she smells WayWoof or because we're so dirty. In a tiny little voice, she says, 'Oh, *why* are you both so filthy?'

This is one of those grown-up questions that doesn't have a right answer. In nine years, two months and three days on Planet Earth, I have learned that when Mum asks one of those kinds of questions, the best things to do are:

a) avoid eye contact

b) hang head (to try and look as if I'm really, really sorry)

c) shuffle feet (I have no idea what this is for, but I've seen Jack do it and it seems to work).

Mum goes, 'Why on earth blah blah blah clothes blah **yadda yadda** muddy dum de dum?'

I go blink, blink, hang head, **shuffle, shuffle.**

Witch Baby goes, '**Duh, duh, duh**, ha HA HA DUHHHH, Mumma, Lilil, WayWoof.'

And WayWoof goes . . .

Gag. Cough.

Pass the gas masks.

Five:
A bit of glitter

Mum hauls us indoors to change out of our mud-and slime-caked clothes. We wash the bits that need washing and wipe the rest off on towels. Mum wants to tell us about her Plan. We've only just moved into the Old Station House and already she's Planning Things. I wish she'd Plan to move out of the Old Station House and back to Edinburgh, but that isn't going to happen. My heart sinks. When am I ever going to stop missing my old house? Mum doesn't seem to miss it at all.

'Now, darlings . . .'

Any Plan that begins like this spells trouble. When Mum starts a sentence with 'Now, darlings,' I always think, Uh-oh.

'Now, darlings,' she repeats, smiling hugely,

'wouldn't it be a brilliant idea if we threw a party to help us get to know our neighbours. Not a huge party. Just a teeny, weeny little get-together. Some drinks, nibbles, maybe a barbecue . . .'

All Mum's awful Plans start off like this. Small. Teeny, weeny. Nothing huge. Then they start to grow and g r o w. Mum gets a glint in her eye and starts making lists. Long lists of food to buy and things to cook. This is because Mum loves cooking. The more people she has to feed, the happier she is. She likes nothing better than making pizzas as big as duvets. She loves

baking chocolate meringue cakes
that are so tall you could sledge
down them. All my friends used
to love coming to my house for
tea when we lived
in Edinburgh.
I had *loads*
of friends there.
Will I ever make
any friends here? I
don't even know if
there's anybody my
age living nearby.
If there isn't, I'll
have to wait till
school starts to
meet anyone. Maybe Mum's Plan to meet the
neighbours isn't such a bad idea. Just so long as
she doesn't overdo it.

'Mind you, Lily, I've always fancied trying that recipe for suckling pig and that's supposed to feed forty, so . . .'

See? She's overdoing it. We haven't even un-packed our stuff from Edinburgh yet. I don't know where all my books are, Jack's lost his CDs and Dad can't find his stinky old train-ers. We are all hoping Dad *never* finds his stinky old trainers. Secretly, we are all hop-ing that the removal men ate

them. But the point is, we can't even find our *important* stuff, yet there's Mum going on about unimportant stuff like candles, flowers, napkins, tablecloths, a big white tent in the back garden . . .

I have to make her stop.

'Muuum.'

She stops and blinks at me as if she's never really seen me before. The glint in her eyes fades away and she looks like Mum again.

'Heavens, Lily. Whatever was I thinking of? We want to *meet* the neighbours, not marry them. Let's just have a cheese-wine-bread-crisps-and-dips kind of party. A quiet little get-to-know-our-neighbours party. What d'you think, Lil?'

Sounds good to me. I love parties. I love dressing up and staying up late. Then I remember that because we've moved house, I won't *know* anyone at this party. Maybe there won't even *be* anyone there that's my age (nine). **Aaaagh**. A grown-ups only party? That would be awful. Grown-up parties are no fun at all. What *I* want is a proper party. Proper paties have cake,

balloons and conjurers. At proper parties, someone is always sick. Sometimes, after a proper party, my friends are allowed to stay for a sleepover.

Then I remember all over again. We have moved house. We don't live in Edinburgh any more. This time, there's no way Ally, Jen and Frieda are going to stay for a sleepover after the party. Not when they live more than two hundred miles away. I miss my friends so much it makes my throat hurt and my eyes prickle. Suddenly the party doesn't feel like such a great idea after all. I don't want to get to know lots of *new* people. I was perfectly happy with the people I *used* to know. But Mum knows this. She doesn't need to hear me say it all over again. Just like I don't need to hear Dad's list of reasons why we had to move here all over again.

Money.

Jobs.

Houses.

Schools.

Somewhere for me to practise playing my embarrassingly loud musical instrument[*] without the neighbours complaining.

I look up. Mum is staring at me. Did she just ask me a question?

[*] Don't ask.

'Um, right,' I guess. 'The party? Mmmm. Sounds . . . great.'

'And?' Mum rolls her eyes. 'I knew you weren't really listening. What I said was, I need your help, darling. First of all, I thought you and Daisy could help me make some party invitations.'

Daisy's the first to tell Mum what she thinks of that for an idea.

'**Hahahahaha POOOO**,' she mutters,

toddling off into the kitchen.* WayWoof heaves a huge sigh and follows behind. Time for a quick pit-stop. Lucky Mum.

A little later, we get down to the business of making party invitations. Pretty soon, there's a damp and gluey pile of invitations drying on the kitchen table and an unspeakable nappy in the dustbin.

Daisy now looks as if she's been dipped in glue and rolled in glitter. Every bit of her shines and sparkles. She looks exactly like a small and grubby Christmas tree decoration. She looks really sweet. You could almost forget

* This doesn't mean Daisy thinks Mum's idea is full of poo; it means that Daisy has filled her nappy.

she is the same Daisy who turned me into a slug. I suspect that even Daisy forgets that she's a Witch Baby sometimes. While she was concentrating on making the invitations and covering herself in glitter, she must have forgotten to think about WayWoof. Daisy can only manage to concentrate on one thing at a time, so when she was sprinkling glitter, WayWoof just f . . . a . . . d . . . e . . . d away.

For now, that is. He'll be back, but hopefully not for a while. Because the next stage in Mum's Plan is for Daisy and me to deliver the invitations round all the houses. We will have to ring doorbells and knock on doors and actually hand the invitations over because most of the houses round here don't have letter boxes. No, I don't know why either. The last thing I need when we're handing out our gluey, sparkly home-made invitations is for

WayWoof to suddenly appear by my side. What an introduction.

Hi, I'm Lily. I'm your new neighbour with no friends, and here's my little sister Daisy the Witch Baby, and here's our dog who is actually a wolf crossed with a major gas leak.

Yeah. *Great.* Welcome to the neighbourhood.

Six:

A barking rug

Lunch is peanut butter and Marmite on toast for everyone except Daisy. She has mashed avocado on crackers. Daisy likes eating things that look like they've been dredged out of the bottom of a swamp.

'Mmmm numm,' she says, holding out a half-sucked cracker for me to try.

'Yum,' I lie, adding politely, '*Thank* you, Daisy.'

Daisy frowns. Evidently she was hoping for more. Mum has her head in the fridge so she doesn't see Daisy turn into the Swamp Maiden. I do, and it's not pretty. The Swamp Maiden grins disgustingly as she pokes two stumpy fingers into her wide green nostrils. She rummages around in there for ages, as if she's lost something. For some reason I can't turn away, can't close my eyes, can't do anything except watch helplessly as Daisy the Swamp Maiden gets stuck in. Now she's got her *hands* up her nose, now her *arms*, now she's up to her *shoulders* . . . It's horrible, it's gruesome, but I have to admit, it's also utterly fascinating. Then, all of a sudden, it's over.

There's a revolting squelch and the Swamp Maiden turns herself inside out with a *pop*.

And there, sitting on top of Daisy's half-sucked cracker, is a small green frog with an unmistak-ably smug expression on its face.

Mum closes the fridge door. 'Yoghurt, darlings?'

I look at Mum and I look at the Frog Daisy. How come Mum can't see? Why is it only me who notices when Daisy's doing her witchy thing? Honestly. Sometimes I really wonder if Mum's awake or not. She never notices anything. Well . . . not unless it's some-thing to do with food.

The frog flaps its webbed feet and Mum hands it a spoon and unpeels the top of the yoghurt pot.

'So sweet,' Mum sighs, 'even if you *are*

covered in avocado.' She bends over the frog and plants a kiss on top of its slimy head.

Pop! Daisy's back.

After Daisy has had all traces of green avocado-slime removed from her hair, I put her into her pushchair and go to deliver our invitations. Mum stands at the door waving and blowing kisses as if Daisy and I were joining an expedition to the North Pole.

When we turn the corner at the end of our road, we can't see Mum any more. Somewhere in the distance we can hear dogs barking. I can see a house tucked in behind some trees, so we head towards it. As we get closer, the barking grows louder. And louder. I wonder who lives here. Whoever they are, they don't need a doorbell to let them know they've got visitors. They have something far louder than a bell. This is what it sounds like:

YIPYIPYIP   YIPYIPYIPYIPYIPYIPPETTYYIP
YIPYIPYIPYIPYIPYIPPETTYYIPPETTY!
HOWWWWWWWL.
ARF. ARF. ARF. WOOOOF.

And in the distance:
MiaOwly . . .
YOwly . . .
WeeeooooWWW.

This house is really a home for dogs and cats. I can see furry little faces pressed up against every single window, but there are no humans in sight. There's a sign on the front door saying:

> Lucinda and Henry
> welcome you to
> the doghouse.
> Please knock.

'Er. Helloooooooo?' I call.

On the other side of the door, the dogs and cats bark and yowl loudly.

'Knock-knock?' I yell, staring at the front door as if I could make it open by the power of my eyeballs.

'ANYBODY HOME?' I shriek, stepping backwards into an impressively large milk-bottle collection.

CRASH, TINKLE, CHINKA, SMASHHHHHH.

Great. Good start, Lily. All around, the barking becomes hysterical.

In front of us, the door quivers as something on the other side hurls itself against it over and over and over again.

Ker thudda THUDD, it goes, making the whole door shudder. 'DOWN, Bertie! Oooooh, you bad, bad boy,' squeals a voice.

I have approximately half a second to guess that this voice must belong to Bertie's owner when the door bursts open and I am hurled to the ground by a huge barking rug.

I prepare myself for death unless Bertie's owner can save me. Sadly, Bertie's owner is a tiny old lady who hauls feebly on his collar with all her might, her voice quivering with effort.

'NOOOO! Ooooh, you *naughty* boy. Put her DOWN.'

Bertie ignores this. Bertie has a glint in his eye that looks like he's thinking about murder. Briefly, I wonder which bit of me Bertie will eat first, when Daisy, my wonderful, clever, brilliant baby sister, saves my life.

'TOPPIT BAD DOG!' she roars.

And guess what? Bertie toppits. Somehow, Daisy has made Bertie freeze. Not really *freeze* like an ice cube, but 'freeze' as in 'stop'.

Bertie has stopped in mid-drool, his enormous mouth hanging open, displaying rows of yellow fangs. He looks puzzled and confused, as if he's lost something he was really looking forward to. Almost as if someone has stolen his dinner. Bertie's owner smiles. She doesn't know Bertie is spell-bound.

'Ahhhhhhh. *What* a gooood boy,' she says, adding, 'Such a sweet doggy, aren't you, my petal? He'd never do you any harm. Not really.'

I don't believe a word of it. I think if Bertie could understand English, he wouldn't believe it either. I hand over an invitation and flee with Daisy before the spell wears off and Bertie unfreezes. I run up the road, pushing

Daisy as fast
as I can, try-
ing to put some
distance between
us and Bertie's teeth.
Just in case.

We're still running when we pass a field
of sheep.

'Babababababa, BAKSEEP?' Daisy says
hopefully. I know she'd love me to join in,
but running away from big bad dogs means I
can't stop and sing songs for her. I keep going.
Now we're running past a field with horses

and cows in it. I am red-faced and going *pant, pant, puff,* but Daisy has her thumb in her mouth and looks as if she's about to fall asleep. It's hard to believe that this is the same baby who just saved me from being eaten alive. She may look small and helpless, but Daisy is really quite scary. Not only can she make fridges float, but she can freeze dangerous dogs. **Woo-hOO. – Witch Baby.** Better not get on the wrong side of *her.* Or us. Witch Baby and me. The sisters with the extra hisses. Sisssterssss. WOO-HOO. In between gasps and puffs, I try to imagine what it might be like when I start at my new school. This is something I was feeling a bit nervous about, but not any more. Just think – if anyone is really horrible to me, I can always threaten them with my baby sister.

On second thoughts, maybe not. Somehow, I just *know* that's not going to work.

Seven:

Midges stuck to my eyeballs

We've left the doghouse far behind, so I slow down and push Daisy up a little side road that is signposted:

PRIVATE
KEEP OUT
Guard dogs will tear trespassers limb from limb and spread their wibbly sausagey bits all round the neighbourhood

I made that last bit up. What the sign *really* says is:

PRIVATE
NO ENTRY
TO
VEHICULAR
TRAFFIC

I'm pretty sure that doesn't mean Daisy and me, so we carry on till we come to another sign which says:

Loch Mhaidyn 1km

Walkers Welcome
Access to The Folly, Mishnish Castle,
Arkon House and Four Winds

There's something fixed to the fence up ahead. It's a bright pink letter box with a metal nameplate which reads:

Is Hare a girl's name or a boy's name? I have no idea. I won't find out to-day because Hare has a letter box, which means I can quickly post his/her invitation and Daisy and I can continue on our way.

I can't even get anywhere *near* the next house because it's totally surrounded by a huge fence. There are even spikes on top of the fence to stop anyone climbing over. There's a big gate, but it's tied shut with chains and padlocks. I guess whoever lives there doesn't go out much. They probably don't have many visitors either. There's a rusting metal sign hanging off the gate. It says:

The sign doesn't actually say:

haunted house
Now go away, Little girls, and never come back.

but sometimes you don't have to say things to mean them. Peering through the fence, I can see what looks like an empty swimming pool, and in the distance there's an enormous dark shadow which I'm hoping is Arkon House and not a Real Witch lying in wait for unwary invitation-deliverers. Brrrr. I wish I hadn't thought about a Real Witch, even if she's only a made-up one. Just the thought of her makes me shiver. I look around, but I can't see a letter box anywhere. I'm not going to climb the fence and go up to the house. No way. In fact, right then, I decide I'm not even going to risk inviting whoever lives here to our party.

'No way, Daisy,' I say, to break the silence. Why is it so quiet? Where have all the birds gone? I'm getting a weird feeling, as if I'm being *watched*. It's really creepy. 'Right,' I continue, my voice wobbling just a tiny bit. 'They don't get an invite, OK? I bet whoever lives up there on the other side of the fence *never* gets invited to parties. That'll be why they never go out. I bet they're the ugliest witches ever. I bet they've got big pointy chins, huge noses and are covered from head to toe in *warts*.'

Daisy's eyes grow wide and her bottom lip quivers.

'Toe watts?' she says in a very small voice, adding, 'No likeit, toad.'

Uh-oh. Any second now she's going to burst into tears. Time to go.

'BAA-BAA BLACK SHEEP!' I bawl, and thankfully, Daisy joins in.

'Havva bitta WOOOOO.'

Then I turn round and push Daisy very quickly back the way we came.

The Nose is staring into the fireplace in disbelief.

'Whaaaaaat? Tell me we're not going to let that rude little squirt get away with insulting us?' she demands.

'Get over it. *Everyone* insults us,' the Chin says, without looking up from her knitting. 'When did you last hear the word "witch" used as a compliment?'

'Or "Toad",' adds the Toad, not to be outdone.

'But . . . but . . .' splutters the Nose. 'Oh, *please*. Just one teeny weeny lightning bolt? Or a plague of boils? Oh, go on. She deserves some kind of punishment for being so rude.'

'NO!' booms the Chin. 'She's only a child. How many times do I have to say this? No one

103

ever listens to what children say. Daisy was the only person who heard Lily insult us, so let's just forget it.'

'Well, excuse *me*,' squeaks the Nose. 'Forget it? I'd rather inhale jellyfish.'

The Chin lays her knitting on the floor and stands up. 'Right. If you insist,' she sighs. 'But let the punishment fit the crime. What the child said wasn't *that* bad. You're only *mildly* irritated. After all, steam isn't coming out of your ears, is it?'

'I wouldn't know,' mutters the Nose. 'All our mirrors are broken, so I can't check,' but she rolls her eyes and nods in agreement.

'Right. Here's the perfect punishment,' says the Chin, sprinkling a pinch of dust into the fire.

'What's that, dear?' asks the Toad, who hasn't been paying attention.

'Just a little bit of mild irritation where it's needed.' The Chin smiles, then sits down and resumes her knitting.

Daisy has fallen fast asleep, the lucky thing. Sometimes I wish we could swap places and Daisy could push *me* in the pushchair. I wish we could do that right *now* because I'm tired, it's hot and millions of midges have appeared from nowhere. **Ugh**. Midges are like vampires; they land on you, chew a hole in your skin, roll their mouth parts up into a tube and sip your blood. **Double ugh**. I don't want to think about this because I'm walking through a thick cloud of them. Millions and billions of them. **Triple ugh**. I've *never* seen midges like this

before. Soon I'll be breathing midges, eating midges and just before I start screaming, there will be midges stuck to my eyeballs. I am about to give up and run for home when I hear voices up ahead.

Eight:
Midges drink my blood

'You're a great big lying CHEATER!' yells a voice.

'You're just a bad loser,' says another.

'Am not.'

'Are too.'

Daisy and I have stopped beside a stone pillar that says MISHNISH CASTLE, but I can't see anything that looks like a castle. I *can* see two small figures in a garden. Actually, it's hard to see if it's one figure or two, because they're rolling around on the grass, kicking and punching each other and screaming their heads off.

'I HATE you. I hope your head explodes and your eyes go **SQUISH** and, and— Aaaargh OWWWW!'

'Oh, do shut up, Annabel, you big baby.'

'Horrible, snotty big CHEATER, why don't you pick on someone your own size—!'

I still can't make out a castle but now I'm close enough to see that the voices belong to a boy and a girl. They aren't much bigger than I am, but they are a lot crosser.

'You're a big BULLY, Jamie. I'm going to tell Nanny.'

'She won't believe you.'

Annabel is bright red with rage and Jamie

is pale and furious. For some reason they've stopped fighting. They're picking themselves up and . . . uh-oh. They've spotted Daisy and me.

'Oh, hello,' the girl says politely. 'Sorry. We didn't hear you arrive.'

The boy sounds a lot grumpier. 'Do we know you?' he demands.

'**AhhhRRRKKKch**,' I manage because I have just swallowed a mouthful of midges. In between coughs and splutters and choking sounds, I hand them an invitation. This is so embarrassing. I'm bright red, my eyes are streaming, and in between wheezes I am picking midges out of my mouth. The girl glances at her watch and the boy stares at me, frowning slightly. I guess they want Daisy and me to disappear so that they can get on with their fight.

By the time Daisy and I are back on the road, I've been proved right.

'Don't CARE. You ARE a poo-head. Go and TELL Nanny.'

'I will too. And then you'll be in BIIIIG trouble . . .'

Their voices fade away. Daisy has woken up and is gazing at me with big green eyes. I notice that there isn't a single midge anywhere near her. So unfair.

'Tubble tubble, big tubble,' she mutters, frowning balefully at me. Just as I wonder what I've done now, Daisy takes a deep breath and blows hard.

Instantly, my hair streams backwards from my head and the trees overhead thrash around as if there's a storm brewing. Dust fills the air so I have to shut my eyes, but then, just as quickly as it appeared, the wind drops. When I open my eyes, the midges have all gone.

Huh? I peer at Daisy, but she's sucking her thumb as if nothing out of the ordinary has happened. I'm about to say something when four enormous windmills suddenly loom up from behind the trees. Gasp. Even Daisy is impressed.

'*Oooh*,' she says, and I have to agree.

OOOOH. The windmills are HUGE. The stalk of each one is as tall as our house, and the spinny bits that stick out from the middle are each as long as our car. There are four of them, one at each corner of the garden of Four Winds, standing like silent giants s . . . l . . . o . . . w . . . l . . . y waving their arms. Daisy is clapping her hands as if the windmills have just done something very clever and she's applauding them. At least, I *hope* that's what she's doing. A little voice in my head reminds me that sometimes Daisy claps her hands to make things float through the air towards her, but surely she wouldn't do that to a windmill?

Then I become aware that Daisy and I are not alone. I get a sort of prickly feeling, as if a small hedgehog is tiptoeing round the back of my neck, and I spin round to find I'm

being stared at
by a small boy with
his finger firmly wedged
up his nose. **Eeewwww.**
Gross. Small boys can be so
revolting. This one smells like he might
have done something horrible in his
nappy as well. **Eughhhh.**

The small child slowly takes his
finger out of his nose and gapes at me.
To my dismay, he keeps on opening
his mouth. Wider. Wider and wider until his face becomes a giant
mouth surrounded by a rim of
small boy. Once he has turned
his entire face inside out, he
lets rip:

'WAAAAAAAAAAAAAAAAA.'

Wow. That's *loud*. This little boy is probably Four Winds' doorbell.

'Erm,' I say, 'is your mum in?'

The *waaahs* grow louder. Maybe he misheard me. Maybe he thought I'd said, **Fee, fi, fo, fum, what's that smell, is that your bum?**

Or even, **Be he small or be he smelly, I put nose-pickers in my belly.**

Whatever he thought I'd said, he is now roaring so loudly you could moor him offshore and use him as a foghorn.

As a doorbell, though, he works perfectly.

Nine:
The Hiss strikes back

The Chin wakes out of a dream. She must have fallen asleep by the fire, she decides, rubbing her eyes and peering into the flames to work out if she's been asleep for long. What she sees makes her nearly scream out loud. There, appearing in the smoke, is a young girl with long red hair, a young girl who is staring straight at her as if she can read the Chin exactly like you would read a book.

Inside the Chin's brain, alarm bells sound and sirens go

off. This red-haired girl spells *trouble*. Instinctively, the Chin knows that this girl is another one of those pesky, weird children. Just like the Witch Baby's sister, here is another one who can see. Something has to be done, the Chin decides. There's no time to think. Only time to act. Right now, before it's too late.

The door of Four Winds flies open and a girl runs out, heading for the Human Foghorn.

'Wheesht, Mull,' the girl says.

At least, I *think* that's what she said. I'm just wondering what language she was speaking when she turns to me and says, 'Don't worry. He's always wailing his head off.'

'What's his name?'

'Mull,' the girl says glumly. 'My mum's mad about Scottish islands. Mull's twin is called Skye.'

Ah. This rings a bell. I know a little bit about mums and their fondness for mad names. Dad once told me that I was nearly called Tuberose Lupin MacRae. I smile at the girl and say, 'My mum's mad about flowers, so I'm called Lily and this is my little blister, Daisy.' As I speak, my mind is whizzing off in another direction entirely. What on earth could her name be? The only Scottish islands I can think of have names like Rum, Eigg and . . . Muck. Surely her mum couldn't be that cruel. Could she? Then she tells me.

'Aye, but I'm called Vivaldi.'

'I'm sorry?' I gasp, before I can gag myself.

'I know. That's not a Scottish island. It's a dead famous, dead composer. My dad's got some pretty weird ideas for names too. Still, Vivaldi's not that bad. Could be worse. Could be a lot worse. My wee sister's called Mozart.'

'Wow,' is about as much as I can say. I'd love to say, *Oh, poor you. Are your parents mad*? but I know that would be very rude, so I don't. In the huge silence that follows, Vivaldi frowns and begins to root around frantically in her pockets. I can't help noticing that she does have rather a lot of pockets: two at the front and two at the back of her jeans, one on the outside of both legs, two on her shirt and at least eight on her jacket. I also can't help noticing that Vivaldi's search through her pockets is growing more and more desperate.

'Er . . .' I begin, just as she tears off her jacket. For a second I am utterly confused. What *is* she doing? Vivaldi looks up and her face is red with the effort. Off comes her shirt, then her T-shirt.

'It's a bee or a wasp or something. AOWWWW!' she gasps, and suddenly I get it. Something's *stinging* her.

'OWOWOW!' Vivaldi wails, slapping herself on her stomach. 'Oooya wee *monster!*'

Off come the trousers and there, right in the middle of her tummy, is the most enormous wasp I have ever seen, with its stinger buried in Vivaldi's navel.

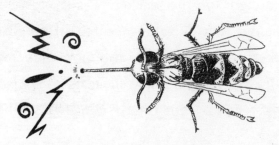

*

Even the Sisters are impressed.

'A *hornet*? Boy, that's *really* going to hurt. I thought you said only a *minor* irritation.' The Nose is taken aback by this dramatic turn of events.

'Shut *UP*,' hisses the Chin. 'The minor irritation was the *midges*, you doughball. But now . . . well. Now everything's changed. Now we have a major problem and a hornet was the only thing I could think of

121

at such short notice. This . . . this Vivaldi child has to be kept away from our Witch Baby.'

'Dare I ask why, Sister dear?' says the Nose.

'*No*,' snaps the Chin. 'Now, out of my way. I have work to do. This is a *disaster*. There was a *one in a million* chance that *another* blue-moon child would come along. One in a *million*! I thought that meant our secret was safe. Oh, how *wrong* I was! Now there are *two* blue-moon children. If they become friends, *anything* could occur. I can't believe this is happening. I am sorry to say that the Plan has changed. *Everything* has changed. Pack your kit, sisters. We're going in.'

I hardly know Vivaldi, but already I know that I want to be her friend. If I'd had to pull a wasp out of my navel, I'd still be crying, but not Vivaldi. Daisy is crying, so is the little boy on the doorstep, but Vivaldi rubs her eyes and manages a watery smile. There's a horrible purply-red lump on her tummy.

'**Phwoarrrr**,' she says. 'What an introduction, eh?'

'Are you OK?' is all I can think of to say.

'Are *you*?' she replies, and then bursts out laughing. 'First time you meet me and I begin by tearing off all my clothes. How embarrassing is *that*?'

I like Vivaldi even more. I like her so much my tongue curls up into a knot and I can't get a single word out. Great.

I can smile, though, so I smile as hard as possible, hoping that Vivaldi doesn't think I'm a complete twit.

'Look,' she says, 'I'm really sorry, but I've got to go now.'

She tosses her head as she speaks and I notice that she's got really long red hair which she's tied up into a knot at the back of her neck. The knot is held in place with what looks like a paintbrush. Not the kind of paintbrush for painting walls – the kind for painting pictures.

'It's a pain,' she says, and then explains, 'My music lesson.' *Toss* goes her head again.

Meanwhile, the waily little boy has grown bored and is edging towards the house with a reproachful look in his eyes. From inside, I can hear another small child letting us all know that it is Very Unhappy.

'So . . .' sighs Vivaldi, 'I'm late. But Mum's in the kitchen feeding Mozart. The door's open. Just go in,' and with a little wave, she runs across her garden and disappears, but not before I notice that she's carrying a big black guitar case.*

So we go in. I have to untie Daisy because I don't want to bump her pushchair up the steps leading to the doorway of Four Winds. Daisy is delighted to be free and wobbles off happily into the house, cooing to herself. I follow behind, just in time to see her opening a door at the far end of the hall. I try to grab her before she disappears through the door, but Daisy's surprisingly fast. By the time I catch up with her, she's halfway across the floor of one of the untidiest rooms I've ever seen.

There are toys *everywhere*. Action Men have camped on top of the refrigerator, a tangle of bare Barbies are bathing in the sink, and the

---

*At least, I assume it's a guitar and that she hasn't got a harmonica rattling around in there, all on its ownsome. Or a collapsible harpsichord. Sadly, judging by the shape of her case, she doesn't play the same deeply embarrassing, loud and weird musical instrument** that I do. This is a great pity.
** As I may have said earlier, don't ask.

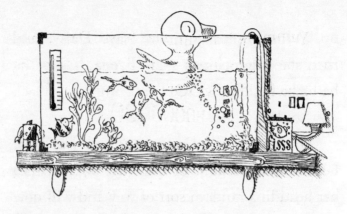

floor is carpeted with a million toy cars. Even the fish tank has a rubber duck floating in it. The only bit of the kitchen that isn't covered with toys is the ceiling.

Daisy looks as if she's died and gone to heaven.

'OooO,' she breathes, and then, 'MMMMmmmmmmHHHmmm.'

For once, I have to agree with her. This kitchen smells delicious. It smells as if someone has been baking. I follow my nose and discover a tray of flapjacks sitting next to the oven.

'Yummayummayumma,' says Daisy, and then she laughs like a small hyena. 'Ha ha ha ha ha ha ha WaYWOOF!'

No. Please, no. NOOOOOOO.

I'm hoping that Daisy only said WayWoof because the thought of him just popped into her head in a random sort of way and will now pop straight back out again. I am *so* hoping that WayWoof isn't about to materialize in the Four Winds kitchen, with his tongue hanging out and a dreadful smell about to erupt from his tail end.

Oh no. No. NO. NO. NO.

It would all be so different if WayWoof was a sweet-smelling dog. Here he comes, picking his way through the toy cars, with a huge, wet grin spread across his hairy face like raspberry jam smeared across a dirty rug. He reaches Daisy and throws himself down,

rolls on his back and prepares himself for a major tummy rub by licking his bottom. Loudly. **Slurrrrp**, **Slurrrp**, **slobber**, **slobber**.

At times like this, I wish he was invisible to me too.

Any minute now, he's going to erupt. Then the lovely smell in the kitchen will turn into a horrible honk. Then Vivaldi's mum will appear, sniff the air, and never invite us back ever again. Time to go. I put a party invitation next to the flapjacks and grab Daisy's hand.

'Come on, Daisy,' I say brightly. 'Let's hit the road.'

Daisy stares at me as if I've said something very rude indeed. Then she heaves a big sigh, as if to say, *How very not funny. Ha. Ha. Ha.*

See Daisy laugh.

See Daisy roll her eyes.

See Daisy glare at Lily.

'Not hit load,' she says and my heart sinks. We've got to go. Before WayWoof . . .

'We have to go home now, Daisy,' I say. 'Mum will be wondering where we are.'

'Not home. Want biccit. Wantit now,' Daisy says, staring at the flapjacks. She claps her hands and a flapjack levers itself off the baking tray and rises into the air.

129

'Daisy?' I squeak. 'That's not your flapjack. Put it back,' but I might as well save my breath. When Daisy wants a biscuit, she wants it *now*. WayWoof begins to fade away because Daisy is concentrating on doing magical things to the flapjack and can't do two magical things at once. I'm concentrating on the flapjack too, because if WayWoof vanishes, then we don't need to go. At least not immediately. We could stay for a while. Meet Vivaldi's mum. Maybe she might offer us some fla—

Suddenly WayWoof springs to life. He jumps up, seizes the floating flapjack in his teeth and makes a bolt for freedom.

Daisy's mouth falls open.

Time to go. I grab Daisy and run.

We're halfway home when WayWoof catches up with us. I notice he's got that stolen flapjack tightly jammed between his jaws.

'Bah dog,' mutters Daisy, but WayWoof and I know that she doesn't mean it. Besides, I'm not even sure that's what she said. WayWoof isn't the only one to have a mouth full of flapjack.

Bah Daisy. At this rate, how am I ever supposed to make friends with Vivaldi? *Hi – I'm Lily, the tongue-tied one. This is my little sister, the Witch Baby, and you probably can't see him, but this is our invisible dog, the flapjack-bandit.*

Ten:
Tasty tentacle treats

'I just don't understand *why* we have to go away for a while. We've *never* been away before,' whines the Toad, her warty lips wobbling in dismay.

'It's only for a short time,' hisses the Chin, cramming another pair of black pointy shoes into her suitcase, then forcing its lid shut. Over by the fireplace, the

Nose is silently wrestling with the contents of a large rucksack. The rucksack appears to be winning.

'I don't believe you,' mutters the Toad. 'If we're only going away  for a short time, then *why* have you both packed so many clothes? I think there's something you're not telling me.'

The Chin ignores this. She is unfolding a map on top of the dining table and propping her reading glasses on the end of her nose. With the tip of one bony finger she slowly traces a path from one

side of the map to the other, nodding as she does so.

'Why am I always the last to know what's happening round here?' complains the Toad. 'Nobody tells *me* anything. It's *so* unfair. I want to know and I want to know now. Where are we going?'

'It's a surprise, stupid,' hisses the Nose, staggering across the room under the weight of her rucksack. 'Now shut up and open the front door.'

'A surprise? Wait a minute. Oooooh, let me guess,' squeaks the Toad, hopping up and down with excitement. 'I get it. No, no, no, don't tell me. We're going to get our Witch Baby? Is that it? Have I guessed right? Is that the surprise?'

Both the Chin and the Nose ignore her completely.

'Did you remember to pack the special crisps?' hisses the Chin.

'Yes,' whispers the Nose. 'I basted them in bacteria last night. If those girls eat so much as one crumb of my **special** crisps, they'll be so **rrrrevoltingly** sick they won't be able to even look at each other again without feeling ill. Plus, the after-effects of eating those crisps usually last three months and will give them breath so rank they'll smell like a cross between a decomposing seal and an old stinky cheese.'

'You are a genius, Sister dear,' says the Chin, shivering at the evil wickedness of their plan, 'but are you sure our Witch Baby won't accidentally eat one of the **special** crisps too?'

'Well . . . I'll admit my plan isn't perfect. But, as I may have said before, you can't make an omelette without breaking some teacups.' The Nose gives a snicker. 'Now chill out, Chin. Our baby will be fine, but the girls are going to wish they'd never met.' She hauls open the front door and braces herself against the wind. 'Come *on*, you two. It's time to go.'

The Toad gulps. 'That's really *nasty*,' she says, swallowing rapidly. 'Just thinking about those poor children innocently tucking into your horrible crisps—' She stops, struck by a sudden thought. 'What flavour are they?'

'What? The children?' snaps the Chin. 'How should I know?'

'No,' groans the Toad. 'What flavour are the *crisps*?'

'I have no idea,' snorts the Chin, picking up

her suitcase and following the Nose out of the front door. 'D'you think I was stupid enough to try one myself?'

Over the next few days, Mum becomes the Human Blur, whizzing round madly, shopping, sorting, chopping, cooking and muttering to herself. Lists appear all round the Old Station House. Lists of Things To Do. Lists of Food Still To Cook. Lists of People To Phone. Lists of Lists.

One morning at breakfast, I notice that there's a list stuck to the fridge with a magnet. The list goes:

1) Get up
2) Brush teeth
3) Have a poo
4) Wash hands
5) Get dressed
6) Breathe in, breathe out
7) . . .

I made that up, but only because this party is driving us all nuts. Dad is the first to crack.

'MEL!' he roars, his voice echoing round the bathroom. I'm in the hall cupboard, trying to find a coat in amongst a pile of crates. So far, all I've found is Dad's shoes and coats and boots. Judging by the smell, one of

the crates is home to Dad's stinky old train-
ers. Holding my nose, I keep looking. The only
coat I can find makes me look like a cross
between a muffin and a furball. I'm trying
hard not to listen to Dad, but he's roaring like
a bull.

'Oh, for heaven's SAKE – this has GOT
to STOP,' he continues, stomping out of the

bathroom so he can roar even louder down the corridor. Fortunately he can't see me in the cupboard or he might roar at me too. There's been a lot of roaring since we moved house. Mum, Dad, Jack, even I roar sometimes. But right now, it's Dad's turn.

'MEL. There's a vast tray of . . . of SOME-THING in the shower. The bath is FULL of bottles of champagne, the sink's got LIVE mussels in it, and frankly, sweetheart, I REFUSE to brush my TEETH in the TOILET.'

He's got a point. How are we supposed to stay clean if every sink,

shower and bath in our house is piled high with party food? No one wants to wash along with mussels, we'd rather not brush our teeth down the loo, and when we said we needed a shower, we didn't mean outside with the garden hose.

Yesterday was far, far worse, though.

Yesterday Mum forgot to tell us that there was a live lobster crawling around the bath.

Yesterday it escaped. My brother Jack may never take a bath ever again.

Did you know lobsters were dark blue? No, neither did Jack. Imagine his horror. He went to take a bath (something he's not very keen on doing), but because he's Jack (Tss, t-sss) and Jack never goes anywhere without his ear-buds (Tss, t-sss), he didn't hear the scrabbly, clackitty sound that lobster claws make as they skitter across the bath until it was too late.

Poor Jack.

He was too busy drumming on the sink with two toothbrushes to hear the Claws of Doom behind him. First thing Jack knew about the lobster was after he'd taken off most of his clothes and was leaning over the bath to turn on the taps. Waving something extremely sharp towards Jack's pants was a creature that looked like it had just escaped from the film 𝔗𝔥𝔢 𝔗𝔥𝔦𝔫𝔤 𝔴𝔦𝔱𝔥 𝔓𝔦𝔫𝔠𝔢𝔯𝔰 𝔣𝔯𝔬𝔪 𝔓𝔩𝔞𝔫𝔢𝔱 𝔜𝔬𝔴𝔴𝔴𝔩.

None of us had any idea Jack could squeal that high.

The lobster has gone now. Poor lobster. Mum cooked it yesterday. Now it's in the fridge – along with enough food to feed the Loch Mhaidyn Monster, his Monster wife and all their little Monsters. No matter what else happens at the party tonight, nobody will starve. But even though it seems our house is filled to bursting with food, Mum is still cooking. When is she going to stop? Can't she see we've all had enough? Or, in my case, not nearly enough. I'm ravenous. Everywhere I look, there are tottering piles of food. Food that none of us is allowed to touch till tonight. Dad grabs his toothbrush and storms into the kitchen. I follow close behind.

'THIS IS RIDICULOUS!' Dad roars. 'It's only a party, for heaven's sake, but it's taking over our lives. We don't even *know* these people we've invited. Probably half of them will be ancient, toothless witches and the rest will be on diets. They won't be interested in all your mountains of food . . .'

Uh-oh. Mum puts down the spoon she was stirring with and turns to face Dad. There's a look on her face that makes me come out in goose pimples. She puts her hands on her hips and takes a big deep breath. **Uh-oh.** Here comes **The Roaring**. If I was Dad, I'd start running now. Except he can't run because I'm the only one who knows where his stinky trainers are, and I'm not going to tell.

In the middle of all **The Roaring**, Jack and Daisy are ignoring Mum and Dad completely and eating breakfast. This seems like a good idea. I grab the biggest bowl I can find and pour myself some Ricey Krispettes. I check. Mum is still **Roaring** at Dad, so she doesn't notice as I pour some of her

favourite Honey Puff Pillows on top of the Ricey Krispettes. Mmmm. I check again. Dad is **Roaring** at Mum. Quick. I dump the last of Dad's super-deluxe-eyewateringly-expensive Blueberry and Dark Chocolate Praline Clusters on top of the Honey Puff Pillows and Ricey Krispettes and drown the lot in milk. Yum. YUM YUM. 'Ooooooooo, Lilililililililily,' Daisy breathes.

I jump guiltily. **Uh-oh.**

'Baaaaaadlily. Nottynottynotty,' mutters Daisy.

Just then, **The Roaring** stops. Mum and Dad kiss and make up. Peace at last. And nobody noticed me piling cereals into my bowl. I turn to Daisy and stick my tongue out at her. Daisy thinks this is hysterical and splutters and chokes on her cereal, spraying a mouthful of ToastyOatys straight across the kitchen table

and onto Jack's toast. Being Jack, he doesn't notice. T̶s̶s̶s̶, t̶s̶s̶ go his earbuds.

Double **eughhh**.

Daisy notices, though. She stares at the blob of breakfast cereal she sprayed onto Jack's toast and gives a little smile. The breakfast-cereal blob quivers and wobbles as if it's alive. Oh, no. It is alive. It sprouts tiny tentacles and waves them

cheerily at Jack as if to say, *COOOOOEEEE,*
Jack. Lookeee here. On your TOAST, but Jack
doesn't notice.

Daisy heaves a sigh and narrows her eyes.
Now the breakfast-cereal blob is lurching
across Jack's toast, dragging itself along
the buttery surface with its tentacles,
lurrrch, slither, flopp, lurrrch, slither, flopp.

I watch as Jack reaches out from behind
the music magazine he's reading, tsss, tss,
fumbles blindly for his plate, tsss, tss, finds
his toast and, still without looking, tsss, tss,
takes a huge bite and puts it back on his plate.
TsSS, tss.

I check. I have to.

Yup. The blob has gone. There's one left-over tentacle dangling from the side of Jack's mouth but it doesn't appear to be moving any more. T̶s̶s̶s̶,̶ ̶t̶s̶s̶.

I check again.

Nope. Not a flicker. He didn't notice that

there was a Witch Baby Tentacle Treat on his toast. Tsss, tss.

Wow. Triple **eughhh**.

Eleven:
My brother, the hard-boiled egg

My bedroom at the Old Station House is upstairs, next to Daisy's. For the second time today, I'm supposed to be changing into something that Mum hopes will make me look like a Proper Girl rather than what she calls a Tomboy. Why does putting on my comfy old jeans turn me into a Tomboy? When Jack puts on *his* comfy old jeans, nobody calls *him* a Tomboy. Or even a Tomgirl. No one pays any attention to what Jack wears, but Daisy and I have to look perfect.

The first time I went upstairs to change, I found Mum had left some clothes out on my bed. I think she was trying to be helpful. I think the clothes on my bed were *suggestions* for what I might want to wear. I looked

at the clothes, but they were all too girly. I'm hoping Vivaldi will be coming to the party so I pretended I hadn't seen Mum's 'suggestions'. Making friends is hard enough without looking like your mum has chosen your clothes. I dug out my favourite shorts and a day-glo blue T-shirt from under my bed.

Mum wasn't impressed.

'Ohhh, Lily,' she said in her Very Disappointed voice.

Bother. *Not* the shorts and T-shirt, then. I went back upstairs and changed into my comfy old jeans and a flowery T-shirt that's a bit small but I love it anyway.

Double bother. She didn't like that either.

It's *so* unfair. I don't like what *she's* wearing, but do I say, 'Ohhh, Mum?'

I don't, but Mum does.

'Ohhh, Lily,' she sighs. '*No*, darling. I know you love your jeans and you practically live in that T-shirt, but tonight is . . . special. Tonight we're all going to dress up.'

We are?

We are.

Just then, Jack appears in the kitchen. My mouth falls open. Jack's face is bright pink. He looks really, really embarrassed. This is understandable. If I looked like him, I would be too. What happened to his *hair*?

'Oh, JACK,' Mum gasps. 'What? Have? You? DONE?'

Behind him, Dad appears, his arms full of shopping, his eyes fixed on Mum as if he's trying to make her be quiet with special Shut-Up-Darling rays beaming out of his eyeballs.

'Mel . . .' he breathes.

'Ohhh, *Jack*,' Mum gasps.

'What?' Jack demands. 'What is it, Mum?'

Silence falls. So, too, does the whisk in Mum's hand. Clatter, clatter, boing boing boingy, sproink, it goes, bouncing across the floor and rolling under the table.

'Jaaaaaack,' Mum wails. 'Ohhhhh, Jack.'

'WHAT?' roars Jack.

'Oh, *Jack*,' Mum sniffs. 'Jack . . .'

'WHAT?' Jack shrieks.

'Oh, JACK.' Mum's hands fly up to her face.

'WHAAAAAAT?'

Enough.

This could go on for ever. For a second I imagine myself grown up, coming back home to visit my family. They will still be living here; in fact they will still be standing in the kitchen but they'll be a lot older. I imagine I can hear their voices: Mum and Dad's will be wobbly and old and Jack's will sound all deep and grown up. Just for fun, I imagine Daisy with chin warts, long black hair and Witch Babies of her own, but not much else will have changed.

'JAaAaAck . . . oh, JaAaAaAck,' Mum will quaver, leaning on her walking stick.

Jack will adjust his tie and peer down at this little white-haired old lady.

'Yes, Mother? What is it now?'

'Jack. OhhHhHhHh, Jack.'

'WHAAAAAAT?'

Back to the present.

Daisy joins in.

'Dack. Ohh, Dack,' she squeaks. 'Hair all gone 'way. Poor hair.'

I agree. Poor, poor hair. Jack's poor hair will probably all have been swept up and dumped in the hairdresser's dustbin by now. He's *bald*. He's got the worst haircut I've ever seen. What was he thinking of?

'WHAT?' Jack roars again. 'It's not *my* fault I look like this. It was *your* idea, Mum.'

'WHAAAAAAT?' Now Mum's doing it too. 'What idea?'

'The haircut,' Dad explains. 'You suggested Jack had his hair trimmed for the party. But it all went a bit wrong.'

'No kidding,' muttered Jack. 'The barber went mad with the clippers. I look like a hard-boiled egg. Talking of which, is there anything to eat? I'm *ravenous*.'

Ten minutes and three peanut butter sandwiches later, Mum and Dad are moving so fast they've turned into the Two-Head-ed Human Blur. Jack's upstairs trying to find a disguise for his newly shaven head – a hat, a scarf, a headband, a new head . . . Daisy's getting ready for her bath[*] and I'm trying to find something to wear. Again.

I refuse to wear Mum's 'suggestions', but I'd probably better not wear my shorts or jeans either. What am I left with?

A long black velvet dress out of the dressing-up box.

My old school uniform.

Tough choice. I'm standing on one leg thinking about this when the doorbell rings.

Aaaaargh. First guest and I'm still in my underwear.

*This means she's selecting which one of her Barbies she intends to drown tonight. This also means she is running around with no clothes on. This means she is not wearing a nappy. Uh-oh. Beware of the damp patches.

Twelve:
Eyes in the back of my head

I am so cross.

The first guest turned out to be Vivaldi. Her mum had sent her round to our house to see if we needed help getting everything ready for the party. We all needed help – me, Jack, Daisy, Mum *and* Dad, but unfortunately, Mum asked first. *Then*, when Vivaldi had finished helping Mum lay out all the glasses, plates, cups and bowls, Dad appeared and asked her to help *him* wrap tons of knives and forks and spoons in rolled-up napkins. Just when I thought Vivaldi had finally finished and could come up to my room and help me choose what to wear, Mum sent me upstairs to look after Daisy and help her into the bath.

I can hear our house filling up with people. I can't leave Daisy on her own, so I'm stuck in the bathroom while, on the other side of the door, there's a party going on. I can hear loads of unfamiliar voices, but I can't hear Vivaldi. I have no idea where she's gone. I need to go and find her, but I can't do that until I've got Daisy out of the bath and into her pyjamas. This is taking for ever.

If I don't get a move on, Vivaldi will go home and all the food will be gone. I don't want to spend the whole party stuck in the bathroom so I'm trying to persuade Daisy that it's time to get out but she won't budge. In fact, Daisy's getting really annoyed with me.

'Nonononono,' she yells, grabbing an armful of Barbies and giving me the 𝕲𝖑𝖆𝖗𝖊 𝖔𝖋 𝕯𝖔𝖔𝖒. I'm ignoring her bad mood. Actually, I'm in a bad mood too, because so far I haven't had one single minute alone with Vivaldi. How am I supposed to make friends with her at this

party if I have to spend the whole time persuading my baby sister to get out of the bath?

'Come *on*, Daze,' I say, reaching forward to pluck her from the water. She slithers out of my grasp like an eel.

'Go WAY, Lillil,' she mutters, turning one of her Barbies' heads right round till it's facing backwa—

AAAAAAAARRRRRGH. No. **NO.** She couldn't have. Daisy? DAISY? I turn to face her. To do this, I have to turn my whole body round until my back is facing her. That way, I can see her, because thanks to her, my head is now the wrong way round. MY HEAD IS ON BACK-TO-FRONT.

This is *awful*. This is a million times worse than being a slug, or having a fridge dropped on your head. Daisy has really Done It this time. I am so shocked, my legs have gone all wobbly. I am going to have to sit down on the floor at once. From outside the bathroom comes the sound of an argument.

'You're a fat pig, Jamie. You ate that whole chocolate cake. That's why you feel so ill. *I'm* only going to eat one or two crisps.'

'Shut up, Annabel. Get out of my way. I need the bathroom – I think I'm going to be sick.'

Yikes. I recognize those names. It's the un-friendly posh kids from Mishnish Castle. To my horror I realize that the bathroom door isn't *locked*. Jamie and Annabel are going to barge in and *see* me with my head on the wrong way round. How embarrassing is *that*?

There's only one thing to do. I leap to my feet and sit on the toilet just as Jamie bursts in. It works perfectly. Jamie catches sight of someone sitting on the toilet, but he doesn't really see me because he turns bright red and

rushes straight back out again, going, 'OH!
Good *grief. So* sorry.'

Before anyone else can barge in, I leap to my
feet and lock the door. Daisy squirms around
in the bath to get a better view
of the New Improved Lily.

'Ooooooh,' she decides.
'Lil gonc 'waaaay,' and she
sits back down hurriedly.

There's a knock at the
bathroom door.

'I say,' yells a voice, 'anyone in there?'

'**NO!**' I shriek,
and then, '**YES!** Go
away.'

No one must see
me with my head
on back-to-front. Not

Jamie or Vivaldi, not Mum or Dad. If anyone saw me like this, they'd call an ambulance and I'd have to go to hospital and have my head cut off and sewn back on the right way round. How horrible would *that* be? I have to break Daisy's spell. Right away, before I'm discovered.

There's a little squeak from the bath. It's the squeak that Daisy's yellow plastic bath ducks make if you squeeze them gently. If you squeeze them really, really hard, they go,

QUAAACK.

Daisy loves her ducks when I play with them and pretend to make them talk. She laughs like a drain. I always start the game by giving one of the ducks a little squeeze so that it goes,

Squeak.

Then I pretend to answer.

'Really?' I'll say. 'You'd like to change the colour of your feathers?'

Squeak.

'From yellow to pink?' I'll say, staring at the duck as if it's really talking to me. We can talk for hours, the ducks and me. We talk and quack and squeak but Daisy never gets bored. Sometimes I wish I'd never invented the Duck Game, but right now it's maybe my only hope of having my head put back on the right way round. With a bit of effort – it's as if my hands are the wrong way round – I grab a duck out of the bath and give my best-ever performance.

Squeak.

'Oh, my goodness!' I cry. 'Whatever is the matter, Mister Duck?'

Squeak.

'Oh you poor, poor thing.' I stare at the yellow plastic duck, my brain whizzing as I desperately think what to say next. 'What – what an *awful* thing to happen.'

I risk a peek at Daisy. She's laughing like a small hyena. With any luck she'll soon forget all about her spell. Keep going, Lily.

Squeak.

'Oh! Poor, poor Mister Duck,' I explain. 'Somebody turned him into a lump of yellow plastic. He hasn't got feathers any more . . .' and running out of things to say, I give the duck an enormous squeeze and it obliges with a huge **QUAAACK** followed by a spectacularly rude squirt of water which flies across

170

the bathroom and splatters onto the window with a **prrrrt** sound. It's so unexpected that I burst out laughing, along with Daisy. Brilliant! Daisy abandons the turning-Lily's-head-the-wrong-way-round spell and immediately two things happen. My head snaps back round the right way and poor Mr Duck flies straight out of my hands and up to the ceiling in a whirr of feathers.

Feathers?

'Fy, fy 'WAY, poo duck!' Daisy bawls. Does she mean poor duck, or does she mean duck poo?

Quack, quack, quack!

I look up. Ruffling their brand-new feathers and sitting in a row on top of the shower rail are Daisy's ducks. Now they're no longer made of yellow plastic, they look really sweet, even if they are dropping duck poo everywhere. Since it's raining duck poo, Daisy decides that it's time to get out of the bath.

'Upupupupupupup,' she repeats, lifting her arms in the air. I scoop her up and wrap her in a huge yellow towel. In my arms, she looks as sweet and fluffy as a baby duck.

Quack.

Thirteen:
A quick bite

'What were you *doing* in there?' Jack demands.

I wish I could tell him the truth, but there's no point. He'd never believe I had my head on back to front. Next time Daisy does something like that, I'm going to take a photograph. *Then* Jack'll believe me.

'Have you seen a girl with long red hair? She's called Vivaldi,' I ask, desperately scanning the crowd downstairs for signs of her. All I can see is grown-ups, none of whom I have ever met before.

Jack sighs, reminding me he's been standing outside the bathroom for ages, waiting for us to emerge. This is probably because he didn't want to go downstairs on his own. I can understand that. The house is full of strangers, after all. Where is Vivaldi?

'Come on, then,' Jack says. 'We'd better go downstairs.'

I stare at him. Jack's wearing black from head to toe: black T-shirt, black trousers and an old black tie of Dad's tied round his bald head like a headband. I'm in my long black dress out of the dressing-up box. It's too late for Mum to make us go upstairs and change if she doesn't like how we look. Actually, I think we look quite cool, but no one notices as we go downstairs. We're walking very slowly because my dress is too long and I don't want to trip and fall. Still nobody notices us. Nobody except Daisy. In between Jack and me, Daisy's head is going from side to side as she stares at first Jack, then me, then back to Jack again. We smile reassuringly at her. At least, I *thought* we were smiling reassuringly. Daisy thought our

smiles meant something else entirely.
Her mouth falls open.

'Oooo, look,' she says. 'Lilil and Dack
like vampie. Ooooo. Vampies.'

Uh-oh.

I sneak a glimpse at Jack.

Oh, dear.

Jack glitters. At least, his eyes do. Not with

brotherly love, either. Jack's eyes are dark, red, scary pools. Jack's got hungry eyes. Sadly, I don't mean hungry-for-party-food eyes. Jack's eyes are vampire eyes and we all know what vampires like to eat. Judging by the way he's looking at me, my eyes have that I'm-in-the-mood-for-blood look, too.

'Li-Li-Lil?' Jack's voice wobbles. His red eyes grow wide and his mouth falls open.

Oh, NO.

Those . . . those *fangs*. No amount of tooth-paste and brushing is going to make them look any better. **Ewwwwww**. As I peer in horror at Jack's fangs, I'm running my tongue round my own teeth.

OUCH.

Oh, NONONO.

I've got big pointy fangs, too. All of a sudden I feel awful. I feel as if there's a gale howling round my tummy. I feel as if small lions are clawing their way out of my middle. I feel as if I'm full of broken glass.

Then I realize what's wrong.

I'm hungry. Peckishhhhh.

Rrrrrrravenous.

I wonder if there's any MEAT in the fridge?

Rrrraw meat. Anything, as long as it's not cooked. I'm not fussy. Mince. Steak. Liver. Chops.

Sausages. Chicken. Black pudding . . .

WHAT AM I SAYING? Black *pudding*? I'd rather *die* than eat black pudding. Then I remember that if I'm a vampire, I'm *already* dead. My mouth drops open. I think I might be about to scream, but when I look downstairs I see all Mum and Dad's guests and I clamp my lips shut. Screaming would only make everyone notice that Jack and I have changed.

Heads would turn. Mum would have to pretend that we were perfectly normal. Poor Mum. Imagine.

'**Ahhhh**,' she'd gasp, her hands flying up to guard her neck, just in case we were thinking of biting her. 'Meet Jack and Lily, my dear little undead children. No, no, DOWN, Lily, you've *been* fed. JACK, *stop* that at once. It's tomato ketchup, not blood, you silly boy. No need to be alarmed, everyone. They won't bite.'

Daisy. This is Daisy's doing.

Before anyone downstairs notices what's going on, I have to break Daisy's spell. Again. This is getting to be a habit. Keeping a lid on Daisy's spells is hard work. What on earth should I do? I suppose I *could* remind her about WayWoof but I don't think having him appear in the middle of the party would be a good idea. Not if Mum and Dad want to make friends, it wouldn't. What to do? I can hardly hear myself think because the noise coming up from downstairs is deafening. Everyone's talking at once, loud music is playing – aHA. That's *it*.

'Jack? Lend me your earbuds for a second. Quick,' and before he can say a word, I grab them from round his neck and show Daisy.

'Look, Daisy.' I smile widely. 'Jack's kindly offered to lend you these.'

Daisy frowns at me and her bottom lip wobbles as if she's about to cry. This is hardly surprising. After all, I am grinning down at her with huge big pointy vampire teeth. Of course, if she cries, the spell will be broken, but I hate making Daisy cry. I'd far rather distract her, and that way, make her stop the vampire spell.

'Don't worry, Daze,' I say, wiggling Jack's earbuds in front of her. 'Listen to these. Jack's got teeny tiny people inside his earbuds. If you listen, you'll hear them singing . . .'

Daisy's face crumples. Her big green eyes fill with tears.

'Go WAY,' she wails. 'No wantit eebuds.

No likeit vamPIES. GO WAYYYYY.'

And suddenly *everyone* notices us.

Luckily for Jack and me, Daisy may well be a witch, but she is also only a baby. As soon as she begins to cry, her spell dissolves. She stops thinking about vampies and starts to think about her world full of woe instead.

Thank heavens.

Poor Daisy. Still wailing, 'NO WANTIT VAMPIES,' she is carried off into the garden by Dad. Luckily Dad has no idea what Daisy is on about.

'Don't you worry, bunny,' I can hear him saying. 'There aren't any. Mummy didn't have time to make pies for the party.'

There may not be any pies to eat, but there is everything else you could ever wish for. Jack makes a bee-line for the cakes and I'm about to help myself to a slab of pizza when I spot a familiar figure coming through the garden door.

Vivaldi!

And now nothing can possibly go wrong. Daisy is safely outside, I'm not a slug or a vampire and my head is on the right way round. Brilliant. Time to go and make friends.

Fourteen:
Extra special

The Sisters arrive dressed in their best party clothes, perfectly camouflaged in a noisy crowd.

'Let's mingle,' whispers the Nose, attempting a smile as she weaves through the crush of guests in the kitchen. She is carrying the Toad like a handbag, and at the first opportunity she puts her Sister down on the floor. The Toad is immediately lost in a sea of strange party guests' legs and spends the next ten minutes trying to avoid being stepped upon. The Chin finds herself pressed up against a bookcase, half listening as a Mr Harukashi tries to tell her how the Internet works.

'Forgive me, Miss Chin,' he says respect-fully, 'but I have never before met someone who has not heard of the Internet.'

The Chin's eyes swivel back and forth, looking desperately for an escape route. What on *earth* does this man mean? Having lived on a mountaintop all her life, she has *no* idea what this dreadful human is on about. If only she was back home, she'd throw him on the fire and *that* would shut him up. Where has the Nose got to? She seems to be taking for ever to sneak the **special** crisps into a bowl where they can be eaten by those pesky blue-moon girls.

'Surely, Miss Chin, you *must* know about e-mail?'

The Chin flutters her eyelashes and tries to pretend that *of course* she knows what e-mail is, has hot and cold *running* e-mail in her house, never leaves

home without a big bag of it by her side . . . but
Mr Harukashi is not to be put off so easily. He
seizes the Chin by the hand and begins to haul
her backwards and forwards as if she was a sack
of coal.

'Forgive me, but I *love* this music,
Miss Chin,' he explains,
grinning madly
as he hops from
foot to foot. 'So
good for danc-
ing, yes? You
also like to
dance, Miss
Chin?'

So *that's*
what he's
doing,
the Chin

realizes, stopping herself just in time from turning Mr Harukashi into a toad. Where, oh *where* has that blasted Nose got to?

Someone has hauled Dad's speakers into the garden and loud music fills the air. This is definitely one of the best parties we've ever had. There are candles everywhere, inside and out, and our new house looks amazing – like something out of a fairy tale. A very LOUD fairy tale. I even saw a *toad* hopping around, but there's no way I'm going to kiss it to see if it'll turn into a handsome prince. There's a very old lady with an enormous nose sleeping in a corner of the kitchen, and no one is paying the slightest bit of attention to what we're doing. This is just as well because Vivaldi and I are having a competition to see how many prawn-cocktail-flavoured crisps we can eat in

three minutes. We're timing ourselves with Mum's egg-timer.

Pretty soon we'll move on to drinking something fizzy and green. After that, we'll probably run around and bounce up and down as if we have springs in our heels. Actually, we'd better not bounce. If we do that, we will both definitely be sick. *Not* a good way to start a friendship.

PARTY!

Before that happens, we have to eat our way through a mountain of prawn cocktail crisps. Unfortunately the mountain doesn't seem to have got any smaller even though Vivaldi and I have been steadily munching for ages. When we began this competition, we had to get rid of some weird-looking green crisps that shouldn't have been in with the prawn cocktail ones. The green crisps don't count in our competition, so there was no way we were going to eat them as well. I dumped them in another bowl along with Mum's horrible parsnip-and-broccoli-flavoured crisps. **Eughhh**. I feel as if I've been eating crisps since dinosaurs walked the Earth. I feel as if I've never eaten anything other than crisps. I feel like I'm going to explode if I have to eat anoth—

Bzzzzzzt, goes Mum's egg-timer.

'Righfff,' I say, swallowing with difficulty. It's funny, but I used to like prawn cocktail crisps. Ten minutes ago I loved them. But not any more. 'Time's up. That was two hundred and six. Your turn.'

Vivaldi takes a deep breath and prepares to try and beat my stunning score. I don't think she's got a hope. Her last score wasn't even close. One hundred and eighty-seven. And with each round of our crisp-cramming competition, we're growing less and less hungry. In fact, we're both full up now. To win, Vivaldi's going to have to finish all of the crisps piled high in the bowl. When I look at her, I can tell that she doesn't think she can do it.

'Ochhh, Lily . . . I, um, don't feel too great.' Vivaldi's face has turned pale. Uh-oh. We haven't even had the green fizzy juice yet. Bit early to give up, surely?

Oh, dear. Apparently not.

Pretending to be asleep on the other side of the kitchen, the Nose is watching the crisp-eating competition through half-shut eyes. She is beside herself with glee. Judging by the awful sounds, the blue moon girl must have eaten some of the **special** crisps. Serves her right, thinks the Nose unkindly. Now she'll be ill for days and days, and by the time she gets better, she'll never want to clap eyes on Lily or precious Witch Baby ever again. Lily, in her turn, will never want to see Blue Moon girl again. Not when Blue Moon girl smells like Decomposing-Seal-Crossed-With-Stinky-Cheese girl. For three months, all Blue Moon girl will have to do is *breathe* and flowers will wilt, trees will drop their leaves and grown men will turn pale and run away.

For once, things have worked out perfectly.

The Nose yawns and stretches.

Her work here is done. Time to round up her Sisters and head for home. The secret of their Witch Baby is safe . . . for now.

The Nose stands up. Remembering that she's supposed to be a party guest, she totters over to the table to see if there's anything good to eat. To her horror, she catches sight of something familiar in a bowl. The Nose can hardly believe her eyes.

Lying on top of a pile of ordinary crisps are the **special** ones. The Nose counts rapidly. Not a single *one* has been eaten. Whaaaat? Before she can stop herself, the Nose gives a howl of rage, then rushes out of the kitchen to find her Sisters.

Poor Vivaldi. Poor me, too. No wonder that old lady with the big nose had to leave the room in a hurry. If there's anything I hate more than being sick, it's hearing somebody else doing it.

Eughhhhh. I wish Vivaldi had reached the sink in time.

Just then, Daisy totters into the kitchen. She takes one look at the prawny puddle on the floor and turns pale. Actually, I'm feeling a bit pale, too.

'Woss at?' Daisy demands, wobbling closer to Vivaldi's puddle, all the better to examine it.

Vivaldi groans.

Daisy squats down and peers into the puddle hopefully, as if there might be something w o n d e r f u l floating in it.

'WOSS AT?' she bawls, and I'm just about to answer when a familiar black shape bounds across the kitchen, tail wagging wildly. Way-Woof! He's so *pleased* to see us. Seconds later, his smell appears; today it's extra-cabbagey.

Immediately I have an awful thought. Because WayWoof is invisible to everybody except Daisy and me, Vivaldi will think the source of the terrible smell is me.

She'll never want to see me ever again. And that's before she's even found out what musical instrument I play.* Brain racing, I try to think up an excuse for the smell, but no words come

---

* Like I may have said before, don't ask.

out of my mouth. How on earth am I going to explain about WayWoof? Inside my head, I hear myself make a lame excuse:

It, it's not what you think, Vivaldi. The dreadful smell isn't me. I DID NOT DO THAT WHIFF. Our dog did that. Well, actually, he's my sister's dog. You can't actually SEE him because he's her . . . uh . . . invisible dog—

Oh, *dear.*

Vivaldi won't even look at me. She's feeling better, though. I can tell, because her face isn't pale green any more and she's smiling. Sadly, she's not smiling at me. She'll probably never smile at me again. At least, not without holding her nose. She squats down beside Daisy. Surely she's not about to peer into her own puddle?

'Here, girl. C'mere, girl. Here. Come here, *clever* girl.'

WayWoof's ears twitch and he looks up.

He's obviously torn between sniffing the puddle and sniffing Vivaldi's outstretched hand.

Tough choice.

Being a dog, WayWoof has a quick snuffle in the puddle, then trots across to Vivaldi. With a sheepish expression on his face, he slumps beside her, rolls over onto his back and presents his tummy for rubbing.

'Ahhhhh, you big sook,' Vivaldi says, reaching out to rub him.

Hang on. Wait a minute.

'You – you can *see* him!' I gasp. 'How can you see him?'

'See who? D'you mean her?' Vivaldi ruffles WayWoof affectionately. 'Lovely dog, by the way. What's she called?'

She? But . . . but I thought WayWoof was:

a) invisible

and

b) a boy.

Mind you, everything I know about dogs could be written on one side of a prawn-cocktail-flavoured crisp, but Vivaldi looks as if she's been around dogs all her life. I don't know her well enough yet to ask if she has ever met any invisible dogs before, but if we become friends, I'll make sure I find out. Vivaldi's found WayWoof's ticklish spot behind her ears and WayWoof wriggles in delight, her tongue lolling out of her mouth, trying to lick Vivaldi's hand.

Daisy thinks this is all too funny for words.

'Ahhhhhh,' she coos, reaching up to pat Vivaldi's arm.

Vivaldi coughs and says, '**Phew**, girl. You could use a wee bath, though.'

'Dust hadda baff,' Daisy informs us.

'Not *you*, littly. The dog. She's a bit whiffy.'

That's funny. I was thinking exactly the same thought, but 'a bit whiffy' doesn't even come close. For some reason, WayWoof is extra-super-maxi-ultra-specially pongy plus-plus-plus today. I can smell rotten cabbage, cheesy milk and sweaty sock plus the faintest wisp of **Dead Thing**. **Eughhhh**. Just as I think, *Things can't get much worse*, I hear shouts and shrieks coming from the hall. Vivaldi's eyes grow wide, and Daisy's thumb creeps towards her mouth. I don't dare look, just in case the loud voices belong to people fleeing for their lives from the Real Gate-crashing Witch of Arkon House.

Fifteen:
Totally barking

Thankfully, this isn't the case. There's an old man with a pink face standing on the door-step yelling, 'THE DOGS! **AAARGH!** Lucinda – they're loose! The DOGS are out!'

Then he clutches his chest and sags against our front door as if he's about to fall over. I recognize the lady from the doghouse as she rushes to his side.

'HENRY!' she shrieks. 'What *is* the matter? Whatever do you mean? I locked the DOGS up before I left. They *can't* have escaped.'

Henry takes a deep breath, but before he can say a word there comes the unmistakable sound of barking.

AROOOO. Wurfff=wurff. YIP-YIPYIPYIPYIPYIPYIP!
Uh-oh. This is not good. Wild dogs rarely get invited to parties. We certainly didn't invite them to ours. Mainly because they would eat all the food.

AROOOO. Wurfff=wurff. YIP-YIPYIP-YIPYIPYIPYIP!

They're coming closer. Sounds like a huge number of them. There must have been at least ten of them in the doghouse. YIKES. Ten of them coming our way. Will anyone be brave enough to try and stop them? I doubt it, especially since one of them is Bertie, the rug with fangs. Bertie who wanted to eat me. Bertie who Daisy froze.

AROOOO. Wurfff-wurff. YIPYIPYIPYIPYIPYIPYIP!

Oh, *help*. Can't their owners do something?

'Call them orf, Lucinda,' Henry bawls. 'They'll listen to you.' But Lucinda isn't

listening. She's struggling back into her coat and fishing in her pockets for something.

'BOTHER and blast it. Didn't bring the whistle,' she roars.

Just then, a familiar black shadow hurls itself past me and sneaks invisibly through the crowd. WayWoof to the rescue! She stops beside the table with all the food on it and sniffs. Sadly, it begins to dawn on me that WayWoof hasn't come to rescue us from the dogs. She's come to rescue the food. Great. Thanks a *lot*, WayWoof. Then, all of a sudden, WayWoof seems to become aware of  the not-so-distant barking. Her head comes up out of a bowl of chicken salad, and her ears twitch. She makes a sudden dive back into the hall, just as the dogs arrive on our doorstep.

Before I can say, *Help yourself to the horrible green crisps, we think they smell revolting*, dogs are pouring into our hall to stand in a panting huddle surrounded by shrieking guests.

'No. *Don't* jump up. Baaad dogs. SIT!' Vivaldi roars.

'DOWN, boys! Get DOWN!' shrieks Lucinda.

'HEEL, you brutes, I say *HEEL*,' bawls Henry.

'OUT!' yells Mum. 'Get them OUT!' and then, as if she's just remembered that she's meant to be a good host, even if this includes being polite to guests' pets, she adds, 'PLEASE?'

But the dogs ignore everyone.

They don't even pay any attention to the horrible green crisps.

They bark and howl and bare all their teeth

and look about as scary as it is possible to look without sprouting horns and tentacles. In the middle of all those yellow teeth, I recognize Bertie. He's easy to spot in a crowd, since he's so *huge* his head sticks up above all the others.

Oh, no, no, no. He seems to be looking for something.

Please, let it not be me.

Sixteen:
Starring WayWoof

Over the din of dogs and guests I can hear Mum shouting, 'The *food*. Keep them away from all the food. Get OUT. **Ugh**. **GERRROFF**.'

Then there's a foghorn roar from Lucinda: '*DOWN*, boys. HERE, boys. Come to Mumsy.'

Gosh. Lucinda is so *loud*. Then I hear Mum's blow-the-windows-out roar.

'SHUT THE KITCHEN DOOR, LILY. SHUT THE DOOR NOW.'

Wow. Now *that* was loud. That wa—

'LILY. DO IT NOW.'

To hear is to obey. I spin round to do as I'm told, but I'm too late. A tidal wave of teeth and tails surges towards me. I'm going to die. I brace myself for **Death By Dog**, but to my relief,

it doesn't happen. The vast dog-tide washes
around, over and past me, into the kitchen.

The dogs swirl around the table with their
tails thumping against chairs and cupboards.
Any minute now, they'll work out that there's
tons of food piled on the table. About two
seconds later, they'll eat the lot. Even the
cakes. Dogs don't care – they'll eat anything.

But Mum's cakes are way too good for dogs. Coffee and walnut cake, carrot cake, chocolate meringues, strawberry Victoria sponge, apricot almond cake, plum and marzipan cake . . . I can't bear it. Are they all doomed to vanish down the throats of Bertie and his friends?

WOOF, ARF, YIP YIP YIP YIP!

Maybe WayWoof will come to the rescue. After all, she is our dog. She ought to be defending our house from the invaders,

not sitting down and . . . and licking her bottom. Why is she doing that *now*? That is *disgusting*. She even looks as if she's thinking, *Mmm, hmmm. Yum, yum. My, this is good*.

Obviously, Way-Woof must have failed her How-To-Be-A-Good-Dog exams. I can just imagine her getting the wrong answer to every one of her exam questions.

Q. Invaders have stormed your kennel. What do you do first?

A. Lick my bottom.

Q. Your Humans are in danger and what do you do?

A. Lick my bottom.

Q. All the food in your kennel is about to be stolen. What are you going to do about it?

A. Ooooh, that's tough. Er. I know. Lick my bottom.

AARF, **WOOF**, YIP, HOWWWWWL.

For some reason all the dogs are now gathered round WayWoof in a panting huddle. WayWoof looks up, realizes that she's the centre of attention, and instead of being deeply embarrassed and apologizing for being so revolting, she heaves a huge sigh, bends back down and carries on. Seeing this, Vivaldi pushes her way through the dogs till she reaches WayWoof's side.

'Is your dog in season?' she bawls, over the din.

In season? I had never given it much thought. Do dogs have seasons?

'I suppose WayWoof's kind of summery,' I roar, adding, 'Hot, sticky . . . loads of flies . . . er, why do you ask?'

Vivaldi stares at me, puzzled, then she grabs WayWoof by her ruff and begins to drag her out of the back door.

'I MEAN,' she yells from the garden, 'is Your Dog On HEAT?'

I never have a chance to answer that. The massed roar from WayWoof's ten hopeful husbands provides all the answer anyone could ever need.

AROOO, yip yip yip yip yip yip yip yip, ARF ARF!

All of a sudden, the kitchen empties out. WayWoof and Vivaldi are sprinting across the garden, fleeing the dog pack. All ten dogs are falling over each other in an attempt to catch up. I don't think it's Vivaldi they want. It's WayWoof. She's the dog-magnet. Wherever she goes, the dogs will follow.

'Ways WayWoof?' Daisy demands, adding in a rather cross voice, *My* WayWoof.'

Uh-oh. In a way, she's right. WayWoof is her dog. After all, Daisy the Witch Baby magicked her into life. And if Daisy forgets about her because WayWoof has vanished across the garden with Vivaldi, then WayWoof will simply f . . . a . . . d . . . e away. How could I explain *that* to Vivaldi? Imagine.

Um, yes, Vivaldi, see our dog? Well, then again, now you CAN'T see our dog because she's faded away. That's because unless my baby sister concentrates on doing a dog spell, she doesn't exist.

Our dog, I mean, not my baby sister. Er. What I really mean is . . . um . . .

I can also imagine Vivaldi's eyes rolling backwards in her head as she thinks, *Boy. What a weirdo. How soon can I get away from her?*

There's only one thing to do. I grab Daisy, plonk her in her pushchair and take off after Vivaldi and WayWoof. As we run, I'm desperately trying to keep Daisy concentrating on WayWoof.

'Way WayWoof?' Daisy yawns as if she couldn't care less where WayWoof is. She yawns again. Widely. Uh-oh. If she falls asleep now, WayWoof will vanish.

'NO!' I shriek, then, remembering that Daisy probably doesn't like being shrieked at, I add, 'No, no, no, let's go and find that naughty, *naughty* WayWoof, shall we?'

Daisy's eyelids flutter. She's falling asleep.

Oh no, oh no, oh—

Vivaldi appears round the side of the shaggy hedge between the doghouse and the road. She is alone.

Oh no, oh no, oh—

'Sorted,' says Vivaldi, dusting her hands together in a there-that's-that-done kind of way.

'Where? What did? Who?' I manage.

'The dogs are shut in their own house.' Vivaldi grins, adding, 'Well, no. In their owners' house, really. In the kitchen. Seemed like a good idea. Actually, the dogs went there by themselves. Soon as they arrived in the kitchen, they totally lost interest in chasing your dog. Which might have something to do with them finding twenty-seven saucers full of catfood lying on the kitchen floor.'

'Ah,' I say.

'Or,' Vivaldi adds, grinning widely as she

crouches down to look at Daisy, who is fast asleep, 'perhaps it was when your dog became . . . sort of see-through and then jist kind of faded out of sight. I guess that was when all the dogs jist gave up and got bored. Kind of understandable, eh no?'

'Ah . . .' I manage. Now I'm beginning to blush. Vivaldi must think I'm not only deeply weird, but a total idiot, too.

She'll never be my friend. Not now. Poisoned with crisps, gassed by WayWoof, weirded out by seeing WayWoof fade away, and finally forced to talk to me, the tongue-tied, beetroot-faced misfit. Great. I'm so sunk in misery that I nearly don't hear what she's saying.

'Thank goodness they didn't eat your mum's chocolate cake. Now *that* would've been the pits.' Vivaldi gives a loud snort and slaps

herself on her forehead. 'Ochhh, you must think
I'm just a total beast, Lily. First I throw up all
over your house and now I'm talking about
eating your chocolate cake. I'm really sorry.'
She dissolves into giggles. 'Aw but' – she gasps
– 'it was jist so funny. All those dogs going daft
in the middle of all those grown-ups. And your
dog' – another gasp – 'I don't think I've ever
enjoyed a party so much.'

I feel as if I've been drowning and Vivaldi's

just come along and thrown me a lifejacket. I grab hold.

'Let's go see if there's any left. Chocolate cake, I mean.' I happen to know that Mum baked two and hid one at the back of the hall cupboard. No, I don't know why either. Mum does that sort of thing. Anyone who keeps a live lobster in the bath is quite likely to have a chocolate cake or two hidden up her sleeves. Literally. I wonder if Vivaldi has any idea what she's letting herself in for. Being friends with the MacRaes is . . .

'MAGIC!' Vivaldi roars, and then immediately claps both hands over her mouth. 'Och. Sorry, sorry, sorry. Forgot the squirt was asleep.'

'*Not* seeping.'

Uh-oh. Daisy's awake again, which means . . . any second now . . .

219

Ah, yes. **Phwoarrrr**. The Unmistakable Odour. The Whiff of Whiffs. The Pong of Champions and the Stench of tonight's Star Performer.

Welcome back, WayWoof. I think we might just steal you a slab of cake to say thank you.

Seventeen:
In a huddle with the Hisses

Though the evening is warm, someone has lit the fire in the study at the Old Station House, and the Sisters of Hiss are huddled around it. At the first signs of the coming dog invasion, all three Sisters made themselves scarce. The Sisters have always *hated* dogs, mainly because dogs are renowned for barking at nothing, or at least *that's* what humans think. In fact any form of magic makes dogs feel acutely uncomfortable, and when dogs feel uncomfortable, they bark. Being barked at makes Witches feel uncomfortable, too, and when Witches feel uncomfortable . . . well, anything could happen.

Before the Sisters of Hiss feel so uncomfortable they do something rash,[*] they retreat to the quietest room in the house and cause the door

---

[*] 'Rash' like causing a hurricane to swallow Lily's house and drop it in a neighbouring country like, say, New Zealand. Or perhaps 'rash' as in causing all the dogs to come running back to Lily's house, where they would turn into sheep, stampede upstairs, drop sheep-poo all over the rugs and try to eat the curtains.

to lock itself shut behind them. Just in case any party guest tries to follow them, the Sisters cast a spell on the door which makes sure that anyone who comes near will instantly need to bolt to the bathroom.* Now they sit peering into the fireplace, each of them thinking dark and gloomy thoughts.

Their plan to stop Vivaldi and Lily becoming friends is in ruins. Not only did the girls

*For reasons which do not require spelling out, this kind of spell is foolproof, but can be messy.

fail to eat the special crisps, but the Toad was unable to retrieve them and try again. In fact, she has just seen another party guest eating them. All five of them.

The Sisters stare gloomily into the fire, ignoring the sound of Annabel being noisily sick in the downstairs bathroom.*

'Any other suggestions?' sighs the Chin.

'We could just snatch the Witch Baby now,' says the Nose. 'Why are we waiting?'

'Why are we waiting?' echoes the Chin. 'Because none of us wants to look after a real baby. Remember?'

The Sisters stare at each other in the firelight. The Chin is right.

'Euggghhhh. Nappies,' groans the Toad.

---

* After eating the special crisps, Annabel was instantly sick in the kitchen sink, then gave a repeat performance halfway up the stairs, an encore outside the upstairs bathroom (engaged) a second chance to hear her repeat herself, halfway down the stairs, and finally claimed the downstairs bathroom as her own vomitorium. Sadly it is very hard to feel too sorry for her.

'Cuddly teddy bears and picture books with *happy* endings,' shudders the Nose.

'*Precisely*,' says the Chin. 'Let's not be too hasty here. Let's wait till she's a bit bigger, hmmm? After all, who in their right mind would believe that a baby could have such amazing powers? And for that matter, *who* in their right mind would believe the word of two little girls whose idea of entertainment is to eat so many crisps they make themselves sick? No, dearest Sisters, I think our secret is safe for now.'

'Does that mean we can go back home to our lovely gloomy mountain?' The Nose cheers up at the thought of going home.

'No,' says the Chin. 'Not yet. But I have found a wonderfully gloomy house for us to stay in. It's not too far from here, which means we can keep an eye on our Witch Baby until she's ready. You'll *love* the house. It's got barbed wire and a high wall, but best of all, everyone thinks it's haunted, so we won't get any visitors.'

'Is it dark?' says the Nose.

'As midnight,' says the Chin.

'Depressingly damp?' says the Toad hopefully.

'The walls ooze,' says the Chin.

From somewhere in the darkness beyond the window comes a terrible groaning sound. The Sisters immediately fall silent and strain to hear more. The sound changes to a high-pitched wailing accompanied by a low drone.

'Oh . . .' breathes the Toad. 'That's simply hideous.'

The sound grows in volume. It sounds painful.

'Awful,' agrees the Nose, listening as hard as she can.

Outside, the terrible noise goes on and on and on. The Chin says nothing but closes her eyes blissfully. The sound of bagpipes continues to fill the night with its insistent blare. The Sisters *love* it. The Sisters think the bagpipes sound exactly like the wind shrieking down the chimney back in their house on Ben Screeeiiighe. When the study fire gives out a puff of black smoke, the Sisters smile at each other. Now they feel completely at home. It's all going to work out perfectly, just like the Chin said.

On the other side of the door to the study, the party is in full swing. Lily's parents are delighted by how much fun everyone is having. Lily's dad has hardly stopped laughing all night long, and Lily's mum is dizzy from dancing so much. The house looks as if it's been hit by a small tornado, but who cares? It's a perfect party, on a perfect summer's night. The moon and the stars shine down on the guests dancing on the lawn and everyone vows that they will remember the MacRaes' party for months to come.

It's getting dark as Daisy, Vivaldi and I make our way back to the Old Station House. I'm very glad I'm not on my own because it's darker here than it was in Edinburgh. I'd grown used to streetlights and shop lights and cars' headlights. Here we've got the moon and the stars and a dim glow from the houses nearby.

It's really quiet, too. I can hear an owl hoot from far, far away and something rustling in the shadows nearby. I am *not* going to think about what's making that noise.

With no warning, Vivaldi stops and I nearly bang into her with Daisy's pushchair.

'What's that?' she hisses.

WayWoof has stopped in the middle of the road. WayWoof's fur is bristling and her top lip is curling up to show her teeth.

'It's coming from over there,' Vivaldi whispers, pointing in the direction of a clump of deep shadow on the other side of the road. I decide that I'm not going to notice that Vivaldi is pointing into the shadows with a very wobbly hand.

I peer into the darkness, but I can't see a thing. The shadows are so black I can feel them pressing up against my eyeballs.

'It's prob-prob-ob-obably just a rab-bab-babbit, duh-duh-don't you think?'

Gosh. What's *happened* to my voice? It's shaking like a jelly. How embarrassing. I'm going to ignore the fact that *all* of Vivaldi is now shaking like a jelly. And I'm going to pretend that WayWoof *hasn't* started growling as if she *knows* there's something bad out there.

Uh-oh.

Now Way-
Woof's pointing her
nose in the direction
of where she thinks it is

and her growling is getting even louder.

Vivaldi clutches my arm. 'Luh-luh-look,' she gasps. 'There's some-somethi-thing over the-the-there.'

I don't want to luh-luh-look. Especially not over the-the-there. But I have to. And she's right, there is something over there. I will *not* think about the Monster of Loch Mhaidyn. I will *not*. I clutch Vivaldi. What should we do? Should we make a run for it? We can't run very far and we certainly can't run very fast, not without tipping Daisy out of her pushchair. Oh, NO. Whatever the something that *isn't* the Monster of Loch Mhaidyn is, it's coming closer and closer . . .

Just as I think I'm about to scream, Daisy yells, 'Hahahahahahaha, PEEKABOO Dack!' and Jack leaps out of the shadows shrieking, '**YARRRRRRRRRR**!'

and we all scream our heads off:

'EEEEEEEEEEEEEEEEEEEEEEEEEEEEEEEEK!'

We're all walking home together now. Jack has brought a torch, but we decide it's better to try and let our eyes adjust to the darkness. That way we can see the stars. All of them. There's *millions* more stars here than there were in Edinburgh. Jack's really good at naming them all, although sometimes I wonder if he's just making some of the names up. Like now, for instance.

'Look, Daisy, see all those stars up there? Shaped like a bear's head?'

'Ahhh. See it, Dack.' She's probably making this up, too. Daisy is looking in the wrong direction completely and waving her chubby fists at the other side of the sky.

'Yup, that's right. Well, that's called Teddy Major. If you look very carefully, beside Teddy

Major is a red star. D'you see that one?'

Teddy Major? He's got to be kidding.

'That's called Betelgeuse. It's named after all the beetles that flew there. Betelgeuse has a weird kind of extreme gravity that kind of sucks things into its orbit. It sucks really hard. *Really* hard. Like a humungous vacuum cleaner. Betelgeuse sucks so hard that

any passing insect, or beetle, or even astronaut,
gets hoovered in by the pull of its extreme
gravity and – SPLAT – gets squished flat.'

Daisy looks unimpressed, so Jack adds
in just one more extra-gruesome bit of inform-
ation.

'Squished so flat, all their insides come out.
All their juice . . . That's how it got its name.

Betelgeuse. And that's why it's red, too, from all the blood.'

Wow. **Yuck**.

Vivaldi chips in, 'So, what makes a blue moon blue?'

'*I* was born under a blue moon,' I say before Jack can launch into another of his gruesome stories. Then I add, 'Dad says that if you're born under a blue moon, that means you can see things that nobody else can . . .' I tail off because my face is starting to glow bright red. *What* am I saying? *Hi. I'm Lily. I see things that aren't there. Like Daisy the Witch Baby and WayWoof the Invisible gas leak . . .* **Woo-hOO. . .**

But Vivaldi grins and says, '**SNAP**! Me too. May the twenty-second. I'm nine years, two months, one week . . .'

'. . . and four days old,' I finish. I'm amazed.

I've never met anyone else with the same birth-day as me.

'Er?' Jack has stopped walking and is peering at Vivaldi and me as if we are aliens who've just landed on Earth. 'Excuse me? Did I miss something? What *are* you two on about? Blue moons aren't really blue. A blue moon is the second full moon in a month that has had one full moon already. Or some people believe they're the third full moon in a season with four full moons. However, the moon *has* turned blue when there's loads of dust in the atmosphere, and yadda, yadda, blah, blah . . .'

Poor Jack. He keeps on talking, telling us about blue moons and moons that turn blue. He doesn't know that blue moons are magi-cal, wonderful things, but he wouldn't, would he? After all, *he* wasn't born under one. I think he might go on talking for hours but we're nearly home now. We're so close we can hear the music coming from our party. Oh, dear. It's a kind of waily, droney bagpipey music. Uh-oh. I'm getting a bad feeling here. As we cross the garden, I can see the piper, standing down there by the pond I nearly drowned in when I was a slug.

The piper plays on. My heart sinks. I wonder if I ask Daisy nicely, whether she'd turn me back into a slug? The piper speeds up. My heart sinks even further. He's playing a tune I know well. It's a tune my whole family know well.

It's—

'I know that tune,' says Jack, adding helpfully, 'Mind you, he's playing it about twenty times faster than you ever do, eh, Lil?'

Thanks, Jack. Please, stop right there. But no. Jack goes on.

'Bet you wish you could play that fast?'

Shut up, Jack.

'Never mind, Lil. At least now we've moved here you won't have to go down to the bus stop to practise. No more grumpy neighbours complaining about the din, huh?'

Vivaldi is staring at me. Oh, dear. I look away, pretending to check that Daisy's OK. She is. She's perfectly fine, but I knew that already. Oh, heck. *Come on, Daisy*, I silently will her. *Come ON. Turn me back into a slug. PLEASE. Before Vivaldi asks me The Question. Befo—*

'D'you actually play the *bagpipes*?' Vivaldi looks stunned.

Question is, is she stunned with horror? Terror? Disgust?

Will she ever speak to me again? Or, more likely, will she ignore me and tell everyone she meets that the new kid in the Old Station House is a weird, beetroot-faced, tongue-tied bagpipe-player?

'Really?' she demands. 'The pipes?'

I look her straight in the eye. *Get it over with, Lily.*

'Yeah,' I mumble. 'My grandad gave me his pipes just after I was born. Apparently he said I'd the biggest and best set of lungs he'd ever known . . .' I tail off.

Vivaldi is smiling. 'That's *so* cool,' she says. 'I've always wished I could play the pipes. I think they're *amazing*. I love how they sound.'

Huh?

Is she mad? I've been learning the pipes for two whole years and I still sound like a strangled stag. Every time I tuck them under my arm, all the wildlife for miles around runs for cover. Every time I put the chanter to my lips, all my family runs for cover. How can that possibly be cool? I stare at Vivaldi in complete confusion.

Jack's gone, run off to demolish whatever's

left of the party food. Daisy's gone to sleep and WayWoof has faded away. Now that Vivaldi's found out my awful secret, she'll probably vanish, too. I mean, it was nice of her to say my pipes are cool and that she wished she could play. But I'm pretty sure she's just being polite. She's still smiling, though. Her smile, if anything, is even wider. She's waiting for me to say something.

'Er,' I manage, 'I can show you how to play, if you like.'

Vivaldi tucks her arm into mine. 'That,' she says, 'would be cooler than cool. That would be magic.' She sighs with what sounds very much like happiness and adds, 'And can we have chocolate cake afterwards?'

I look up at the millions of stars up above. Far, far off, on the other side of the solar system, millions of miles out there in deepest space, a shooting star falls away into the darkness. For once, I let it go. For once, I don't need to make a wish.

Ae last Hiss

'You haven't heard the laSSSSt of uSSSS.' The Nose's voice echoes eerily round the empty rooms of Arkon House.

'Oh, do shut *up*,' hisses the Toad from deep inside a crate full of battered cauldrons. She is trying to scrape together something for supper, but since they've just moved in, this is proving to be harder than she'd thought. Mice and rats are in short supply, and even the nettles outside are weedy little things, not fit to grace a Hiss's plate.

The Nose pretends not to hear. The Nose gazes at her reflection in the bathroom mirror and winks. *Not bad*, she decides, patting a silvery tendril of her wig back into place. *Not bad at all.*

'YesssSS,' she hisses. 'Never underesSSti-mate a HisS. Jussst when you thought it was finissSShed, jusSSt when you thought it was sSSsafe, that'sssSS when we'll sSSneak—'

'Oh, do SHUT UP,' snaps the Chin, irritated beyond reason. 'You're supposed to be painting the bathroom black, not hissing at yourself in the mirror like a lovelorn snake.'

The Nose pulls a hideous face, and the mirror immediately shatters into a thousand pieces.

'Great,' mutters the Toad. 'That'll be *another* thing we'll have to replace when we leave.'

'LEAVE?' squawks the Chin. 'Who said anything about leaving? Read my thin little sneery lips. Nobody leaves until the job is done. Understood? Now, stop moaning and come and give me a hand with this thing.'

The three Sisters stand round their new white plastic computer box-thing, staring at it in bafflement. Mr Harukashi donated it to them with his compliments. None of the Sisters has the least idea how to make it work. Somehow, they're going to have to find out. Four hundred years of living in their cave at the top of Ben Screeeiiighe has left them ill-equipped for life in the twenty-first century, but this must not be allowed to stand in their way. The Hisses must learn about computers, cars, electricity, televisions, mobile phones, cinemas, aeroplanes, music, history, geography and hundreds of other things that Lily and her family take utterly for granted. If the Sisters of Hiss want their Witch Baby Plan to work, then they are going to have to learn an awful lot very quickly indeed.

'You haven't sssssSeen anything yet,' hisses the Nose under her breath as she turns the computer on at the wall.

And for once, she's absolutely right.

About the Author

Debi Gliori is the acclaimed author and illustrator of six fabulous novels about the Strega-Borgia family, a series which started with *Pure Dead Magic*, and more than forty popular picture books, including the Greenaway-shortlisted *Always and Forever*. Her picture books are loved for their glorious, glowing colours and carefully studied detail. Her longer fiction has been lavishly praised for its immensely inventive and entertaining narratives. Her wonderful storytelling is combined with intricate black-and-white line drawings to fantastic effect in *Witch Baby and Me*, her first foray into younger fiction and the start of a new series.

Debi was born in Scotland to a Scottish-Italian family, and trained at Edinburgh College of Art and in Milan. She still lives near Edinburgh, where she combines raising her large family with working in her small, private studio in the back garden. In the small amount of spare time that this leaves, Debi loves cooking and gardening.